CHILDREN'S WARD

CHILDREN'S WARD

Claire Rayner

ISIS
LARGE PRINT
Oxford and Orlando

First published in Great Britain 1966
by Corgi

Published in Large Print 2000 by ISIS Publishing Ltd,
7 Centremead, Osney Mead, Oxford OX2 0ES, and
ISIS Publishing, PO Box 195758,
Winter Springs, Florida 32719-5758, USA
by arrangement with Severn House Publishers Ltd

British Library Cataloguing in Publication Data
Rayner, Claire, 1931-
    Children's ward. – Large print ed., Rev. ed
    1. Love stories 2 Large type books
    I. Title II. Brandon, Sheila, 1931-
    823.9'14 [F]

ISBN 0-7531-6120-6 (hb)
ISBN 0-7531-6209-1 (pb)

Printed and bound by Antony Rowe, Chippenham and Reading

INTRODUCTION

By Claire Rayner

Twenty-five or more years ago, I was a young would-be writer, trying to learn how to make my way in the world of books. I was writing for magazines and newspapers and I'd produced a couple of non-fiction books, but story-telling . . . that was a mystery to me. I knew I liked stories, of course; I've been an avid reader since before I was four years old and to this day I'm a pushover for a well-told tale. But how to tell a tale — *that* was the mystery.

So much so that it simply did not occur to me that I might be able to write fiction. But I was persuaded to try my hand. And because I knew that it is a basic rule of the learner writer always to write what you know, I opted to write about hospital life. After twelve years of sweat, starch, tears and bedpans as a nurse and then a sister in a series of London hospitals, I had an intimate knowledge of how such establishments work. I also knew that a great many people love peering behind closed doors into worlds they don't usually get the chance to experience.

So, I had a go. I started to tell myself stories of hospital life — rather romantic, but none the worse for that — only instead of keeping them in my own head as I had when I'd been a day-dreaming youngster, I struggled to put them on paper. And to my surprise and delight I found that publishers were willing to have a go, and gamble on me. They put my words into books — and I was delighted.

But also a bit embarrassed. I know it isn't an attractive trait to admit to, but there it is — I was a bit of a snob in those days. Not a social snob, you understand, but an intellectual snob. I had the notion that stories like these were a bit "ordinary", that what really mattered was Literature with a capital "L" and I knew perfectly well I wasn't writing that! So instead of using my own name on my first published attempts at story-telling, I borrowed my sister's first name and a surname from elsewhere in my family. And Sheila Brandon was born.

Now I am no longer a literary snob. I know that any storytelling that gives pleasure and interest to readers is nothing to be ashamed of and has a right to exist. It may not be Literature, but then what is? Dickens was just a story-teller in his own time, the equivalent of the writers of "Eastenders" and "Coronation Street". Today he is revered as a Classic. Well, these stories of mine are never going to be classics, but I don't think, now I re-read them, that I need blush too much for them. So, here they are, the first efforts of my young writing years, under my own name at last. I hope you enjoy them. Let me know, either way!

CHAPTER
ONE

From her desk in the glass-walled office, Harriet could see the long ward stretching dimly into the shadows, each small bed and cot humped with the figure of a sleeping child. The little boy in the third cot had both his blue pyjamaed legs stuck out through the bars, and for a moment Harriet wondered whether it would be better to leave him in the hope he would wriggle back under the covers later in the night, or whether to risk waking him by moving him now. And then she remembered wryly just how loudly he could shriek when he was disturbed, and decided to leave him in peace.

The senior night nurse moved silently through the ward, checking on each child, comforting the odd ones who were still awake and restless. There was a subdued rattle of dishes from the kitchen where one of the juniors was laying the trolleys ready for breakfast the next morning, and there was a distant heavy thumping of traffic from the main road five floors below. With a soft sigh, Harriet looked down at her desk, at the neat piles of charts, the completed day reports and lists for the next morning, and slowly reached for her white cuffs to slip them over the dark blue sleeves of her dress.

1

It was half past eight, and clearly there was no further excuse she could find for staying on duty any longer. Another day, she thought, another full day of activity, but without a sight of him.

I'm worse than the silliest schoolgirl, she told herself bitterly, hanging around in the hope he'll come to the ward for some reason or other — and even if he did, it probably wouldn't make any difference.

The big double doors of the ward swung open with a soft swish, and with a moment's wild hope, she peered through the glass partition to see if perhaps it had been worth hanging about after all, but the dim gleam of a white cap sent the hope stillborn back to the pit of her stomach.

Sally, soft footed, came into the office, dropping her blue cape onto the only armchair with a grunt of fatigue before sprawling long-leggedly on top of it.

"You busy too? We've been like Paddy's market today — three lists and a blasted ectopic at half past seven. At this rate I'll die of exhaustion before I'm thirty. Why I ever opted to be a theatre sister I'll never know —" She rubbed her snub nose wearily, and peered up at Harriet. "Aren't you finished yet? We're supposed to be meeting them at nine, remember —"

Harriet made a face. "I hadn't forgotten," she said, a little shamefacedly. "I was just finishing off a few odds and ends. I'll be ready —"

"You've been hanging around waiting to see if Weston would come," Sally said accusingly. "Honestly, Harriet, you are a nit! Quite apart from the fact that he was in theatre till seven o'clock and probably won't do any ward rounds tonight, what's the point? It's not as though he ever paid any attention to you — and there's Paul —"

Harriet looked at her, an almost comically guilty expression on her face. "I know, Sal. I'm an ass, I'm an idiot, I'm everything you ever care to call me, but I can't help it — he just has that effect on me."

Sally got to her feet and came to stand beside Harriet at her desk looking down at the bent head with a sort of annoyed sympathy on her round face.

"Harriet love. Listen to me. You've got yourself into a stupid state over this man. You say yourself he never seems to notice you as a person — just treats you with a sort of remote courtesy. As far as he's concerned, you're just Sister Brett, Children's Ward. And for a whole year, you've been mooning around after him as though he were — were Adonis and the Boy David and James Bond all rolled up into one! What's the use? Forget it, lovey. Here you are with Paul ready to lie down and die for you, and all you do is take him for granted! And he's much better looking, and more fun than ten Gregory Westons! Grow up, Harriet, for God's sake —"

And Harriet couldn't argue with her. Everything Sally said was perfectly true, but no matter how often Sally said it — which was very often indeed — Harriet couldn't, or wouldn't listen to her. From the first time Gregory Weston had come to the Royal, as surgical registrar, a year before, he had seemed to Harriet all she ever wanted in a man. Certainly he wasn't as good looking as Paul Martin, the medical registrar, with whom she had, until Gregory Weston turned up, thought herself mildly in love. Paul had fair classic good looks, a cleft chin, the physique of an athlete, a personality that made every girl on the nursing staff shiver delightedly whenever he spoke to them. And Gregory? What was it about him that made Harriet's knees turn to water at the sight of him, made her pulse beat thickly in her throat till she thought she would choke? Lean, not particularly tall — a bare three inches more than Harriet's own compact five foot five — a saturnine face under crisp dark hair grizzled with white. Perhaps it was the fact that he was a good deal older than most of his contemporaries, obviously nearer forty than thirty, perhaps it was the closed face that rarely relaxed into a smile, perhaps the low deep voice with its precise accent — but whatever it was, Harriet loved him.

And in all the year she had been cherishing this ever growing feeling for him he had never made the least sign of regarding her as any more than an efficient ward sister. Harriet's only comfort — and it was a cold one — was that he never paid any attention to anyone else at the Royal either. Most of the other men on the staff had their special friends among the nurses; over the years many of them had married girls they had met around the wards of the big London hospital, but Gregory Weston went his own self-contained way, aloof, solitary, seeming to have no need of any human contact outside his work.

Once, when Harriet had managed to ask Paul a few casual questions about him, when she was at the hospital's annual Christmas dance with him, Paul had

4

said disgustedly, "Old Weston? That man's got ice water in his veins instead of blood. He never joins in any of the mess affairs — pays up like a lamb whenever we whip round for a party, mind you, but goes off and spends the evening in his own room. Look, there're the others — they're making for the bar. Come and get a bit sloshed, and then we'll go and neck somewhere like civilised people —"

And Harriet had gone to have just one drink, and then pleading a fictitious headache, had slipped away, much to Paul's disgust.

Quite what she was to do about Paul, Harriet didn't know. At the beginning, before she had first seen Gregory, she had enjoyed his company, liked his casual love-making after their frequent evenings out together, had even thought seriously about accepting the proposal that her woman's intuition told her would one day come. But all that had gone, melting like snow in the sunshine, and for the past months, she had avoided Paul whenever she could, staving off the inevitable proposal as best she could. Not that her coolness had made any difference to Paul. Indeed, in a way it had made him more ardent. Paul Martin wasn't used to girls who cooled off before he did, and Harriet's arm's length attitude intrigued and piqued him. So he persisted, nagging her till she was forced to accept his invitations. Her only defence had been Sally, Sally and Stephen, the senior pathologist who regarded Sally as his personal property. They were an easy going pair, and didn't seem to mind when Harriet insisted that they made up a foursome with Paul and herself, didn't seem to notice how often Paul was irritated by their presence, sublimely ignoring his attempts to get Harriet away on her own.

Harriet pulled herself out of her reverie, and looked up into Sally's troubled face. "I'm sorry, Sal" she said wearily. "We'd better get changed, I suppose — or Stephen'll think you're not coming —"

"He knows me better than that," Sally said, her face melting into a smile as she thought of her Stephen's rangy body and unruly brown hair. "To tell you the truth, I'm more bothered about old Paul. He's awfully miserable about you, Harriet — and he's a nice chap, really, you know. You could do worse. And to be completely practical, if not romantic, you'd be more than an idiot to let him go for the sake of a starry eyed dream about a man who doesn't know whether you're alive or dead."

Harriet grimaced. "Come off it, Sal. I mayn't be a pocket Venus, but I hardly have to hang on to a man I don't care about just as a — a sort of insurance. There's more to life than just getting married for the sake of it —"

"I'm not so sure." For all her soft round face and pretty ways, there was a strongly practical streak in Sally. "Do you want to spend all your life looking after other people's sick kids? I can't see you settling down into a career for ever and a day. You ought to be married, with kids of your own — and Paul would make a very good husband. And as for not caring for him — piffle. You cared about him before you went all moony and schoolgirlish over Weston. You're just peeved because he takes no notice of you. I'll bet my all that if he once

6

took you out, and you could really get to know him, you'd come running back to Paul with your tail between your legs —"

"Drop it, Sally," Harriet said sharply. "Just drop it. I may be stupid, but that doesn't give you the right to be damned rude —"

"Sorry." Sally said penitently. "It's just that you make me so *mad*. And I like Paul. He's too nice to be a doormat —"

"Come on," Harriet said shortly, reaching for her own blue cape. "Enough of talking — we'd better change."

And Sally, who had known Harriet long enough and well enough to know when to give up, picked up her own cape, and followed her friend out of the office.

Harriet stopped by the kitchen door, and put her head round it to say "Goodnight" to the night nurse, and the two Sisters padded softly along the dimly lit corridor towards the lift gate. Sally pressed the button, and then leaned against the iron gates, rubbing her face again with a tired gesture.

"I don't suppose we'll be going anywhere at all special — Stephen's broke again, and Paul usually is — do you suppose it'll be all right if I just put on slacks and a sweater? That'll do, won't it? And if *you* wear slacks too, it won't matter."

Harriet nodded, peering down the lift shaft to where the cage was grinding its noisy way upwards. "Slacks it is then —" she said, and stood back as the lift arrived and the gates rattled open.

There was a trolley in the lift, with a small shape bundled under the red blankets, and in the corner, a young woman with her face drawn and frightened huddled against the wall, clutching miserably at a little parcel of child's clothes. And next to the trolley, one hand under the blankets to hold onto the invisible wrist of the small patient on it, stood Gregory Weston, his narrow mouth in a grim line.

"Sister!" He seemed a little surprised to see her. "I thought you'd have gone off duty by now — is the cubicle ready?"

"Cubicle?" Harriet stared at him. "What cubicle? I'm sorry — is this patient for my ward?"

He looked angry for a moment. "Didn't Casualty 'phone up?" Harriet shook her head, and stood back as the porter manoeuvred the trolley out of the lift.

"I'm afraid not," she said crisply. "But not to worry. I'll have a cubicle ready immediately." She looked across at Sally, who had gone into the lift and stood ready with her hand over the button. "Sorry, Sally. I'll have to stay. The senior night nurse is new on tonight — it wouldn't be fair to lumber her — explain for me, will you?" and putting a friendly hand on the arm of the young mother who was standing looking unhappily down at the trolley, Harriet crisply shut the lift gates on Sally's exasperated face, and followed the trolley into the darkened ward.

She dropped her cape at the kitchen door, and sent the junior nurse scurrying off to prepare an isolation cubicle at the end of the ward, sent the other junior nurse to settle the young mother in the office with a cup of tea, and hurried down the ward after the trolley and Gregory Weston's lean shape.

"Boy of three," Gregory said succinctly. "Pulled a kettle of boiling water over himself. They're busy in Cas. so I said I'd examine him in the ward — it's cleaner here, anyway. Cas. is full of drunks. Have you a dressing trolley I can use?"

Harriet nodded, and led the way into the far cubicle, where the nurse had just pulled the cot coverings back, and put the heater on to warm the small glass-walled room.

"Bring the emergency dressing trolley from the sterilising room please, Nurse Hughes," she said, "and set up a barrier nursing table outside this cubicle. There's a mask by the washbasin, Mr Weston."

Rapidly, she and Gregory masked and scrubbed their hands, ready to put on the gowns the junior brought with the trolley, and then they stood back as the nurse, at a sign from Gregory, carefully lifted the covers from the child on the trolley, before coming close enough to look down on the small figure that lay there.

He was sleeping the shallow restless sleep of shock, his small arms thrust out to each side of him, red and shiny skin swelling painfully against the sopping wet sleeves of a grubby sweater. By some miracle, his face had escaped any injury, and Harriet crouched beside the trolley, laying her face against one tear blotched cheek to murmur reassurance, as, with the delicacy of a prowling cat, Gregory began to clip the clothing away from the injured area.

The boy whimpered, and stirred, trying to pull his arm away from Gregory's gentle but firm hold, and Harriet crooned softly into the child's ear, watching Gregory's fingers as they manipulated scissors and forceps, easing the fabric away from the swollen flesh and angry red skin.

It took twenty minutes of careful work before the sweater and small vest, cut beyond any hope of repair, were lying on the floor beside the trolley. Gregory straightened his back, and looked down at the child who had drifted off to sleep again as soon as Gregory had finished cleaning the angry reddened scalds. "Mmm." He looked consideringly at the small chest and arms. "Not too bad at all. Lucky little devil. I'll leave the blisters, Sister, for tonight. Just nurse him in the open, and tomorrow we'll have another look and see what's what. I'll put up a drip now — glucose saline, please — and he can have some nepenthe if he needs it. I'll write it up when I've got the drip going —"

By half past nine, the child was settled in bed, a special nurse sitting gowned and masked beside him to watch the slow drip of fluid into the vein in his ankle. The young mother, reassured as much as possible, had been sent home with the promise that a message would be sent if the child's condition seemed bad enough to warrant it.

In the office Gregory watched her go, and sighed impatiently, turning to where Harriet was completing the chart, to reach for the prescription sheet.

"Silly creature," he said with cold anger. "All this because she hadn't the wit to make sure he couldn't get at a kettle of boiling water. Some of these women don't deserve to have children."

Harriet, chilled by his attitude, said sharply. "It was probably less her fault than the fault of the way she has to live." She thrust the chart at him, and pointed to the address on the cover. "Fontana Street. That's a road of houses that should have been condemned years ago — and she told me she only has one room, and a very small room at that. It can't be easy to look after a child properly in those sort of conditions — she hasn't even got a proper cooker. She has to do all her cooking on an oil stove. With a lively three year old to look after, and pregnant again into the bargain, is it any wonder this happened?"

He signed the prescription sheet, and looked up at her under drawn brows. "You managed to discover a lot about her."

Embarrassed, she shrugged slightly. "It's part of my job, isn't it? To know about patients' backgrounds, I mean. It makes a lot of difference to the sort of care they need. This boy, for instance, if he came of well-off parents, the chances are he would be well fed, and in good condition to cope with this accident. As it is, he probably eats poorly — because his mother can't afford to feed him as he should be fed, even if she really understood much about nutrition — and doesn't get enough sleep or fresh air, so he'll need extra vitamins and so on while he's in here — and a long convalescence in the country after he's better —" She faltered. "I'm sorry. You must be tired. I shouldn't waste your time nattering like this."

"You're tired too, I imagine." He made no attempt to go, sitting perched on the corner of her desk, looking down at her where she sat in her usual chair. "I'm sorry too. I shouldn't have been so quick to criticise, I suppose. I — get angry when I see children with unnecessary injuries."

"Don't we all!" Harriet said, and smiled up at him a little shyly. "I didn't mean to sound so sharp — but so often doctors don't seem to know about the sort of lives their patients live outside hospital. It *does* matter."

He nodded, still looking at her considering. "I'm not arguing with you — you had every right to tell me off. How did you know what —" he peered down at the chart "what Fontana Street was like? Is your home around here? I thought all you sisters lived in the hospital."

"We do." Harriet said, "And my home's in Devonshire — but when I got this post, after I finished my training, I thought I ought to know something about the district — so I went around looking."

"Just like that?" he asked curiously. "Just went walking around?"

Harriet nodded. "I suppose it sounds a bit silly, really. But I like walking, and I wanted to know —"

He was silent for a moment, and then he said, with an odd diffidence, "You make me feel a little ashamed. I ought to know more about the district too, I suppose. As you say, it helps when you come to think about patients and their diagnoses and treatment. I just never got around to looking at much outside the hospital —"

Without thinking, Harriet said, "But how could you? You never go out."

"How do you know that?" he asked, his voice suddenly rough.

Harriet's face flamed a hot red in embarrassment. "I — I beg your pardon," she stammered. "I didn't mean to

12

be rude — but — well, you don't, do you? I mean —
well, you never go to any of the parties in the doctors'
common room, and someone once said you never go out
either —"

He stood up, and turned to stare through the glass
partition at the darkened ward stretching into the
shadows.

"No, I don't go out very much —" he said slowly. "It's
a sort of — habit, I suppose. I never seem to get around
to much at all outside my job." He turned and looked at
her, at the fading red in her face and even white teeth
biting her soft lower lip in ashamed embarrassment.
"Does that sound — silly?"

"I suppose not." Harriet managed to smooth her face
into a semblance of calmness. "If that's the sort of life
you really want. But there's so much more to living than
just one's job, however interesting that job may be.
Anyway —" she took a deep breath, and looked straight
at him, her pulse thickening in her throat. "I think you
do a better job if you take a rest from it sometimes.
Unless you really want to live like a hermit, of course —"

Any minute now, part of her mind jeered, you'll be
asking him to go out with you. How silly can you get
about this man, for God's sake?

"Perhaps I do —" For a moment, his habitual grimness
returned, banishing the few moments of relaxation that
had been the first sign of humanity Harriet had ever
really seen in him. But then, he sat down on the corner
of her desk and looked at her again.

"Sister — Brett — Harriet, isn't it?" She nodded
wordlessly. "As you say, I really ought to know a bit

more about the district this hospital is serving. And as you seem to know it pretty well, perhaps you'd spare some time to show me around it? If you aren't too busy —"

"I'd like to," she said, a little breathlessly. "I can always find time to walk — I enjoy walking — it's more fun in the country, at home, but even here, in streets and in all the traffic it's quite pleasant —" she was gabbling a little, so full was she of delighted surprise. "Just let me know when you can manage it, and I'll arrange my off duty accordingly —"

He nodded gravely. "I have a half day this Friday. Will that be suitable?"

She nodded too, and smiled brilliantly. "Fine. I'll be off about two o'clock."

"That's settled then." He got to his feet, and went to the door. "And I'll be up in the morning to see this child again. He may need to go to theatre to have those blisters snipped. I'll decide tomorrow. Goodnight, Sister Brett."

"Goodnight, Mr Weston." Harriet said, and sat in a bemused silence long after the double doors had stopped their swishing behind his departure, guiltily blessing the child whose scald with a kettle of boiling water had made her so happy.

CHAPTER
TWO

Harriet was perched on top of a ladder sorting through the top shelf of the linen cupboard when Sally put her head round the door.

"Hello," Harriet said absently. "Fifteen nightgowns — five bibs — honestly, I think those babies must eat them. We've lost nineteen since the last inventory."

"The nurses probably use 'em as dusters, if your lot are anything like mine. I've lost six dressing towels since the last count. But at least I've finished my inventory. Why are you so late with yours?"

"We do work here sometimes," Harriet said. "I've had three babies with pneumonia this last week, on top of all the usual surgical stuff — I haven't had time." She put the last pile of clothes back on the shelf, and came down the ladder to make a note in the linen book. "Now, what can I do for you? I haven't had a chance to get the list for tomorrow straight yet, so if that's what you're after you'll have to wait. I'll do it after lunch."

"No —" Sally grinned. "I'm off tomorrow, so the list'll be Staff Nurse Baker's headache. I want to know what's happening tonight — if you don't mind my asking," she finished sarcastically.

"Oh — tonight." Harriet led the way out of the linen cupboard, and Sally followed her into the ward. They picked their way over the small groups of children playing on the floor, dodging an active game of tag played by two small boys both of whom had one eye covered with a bandage, an affliction that seemed to hamper them not one whit. Harriet scooped a diminutive child up from an absorbed game of scribbling on the floor and with a pat on his pyjamaed behind sent him off to the lavatory, correctly interpreting his wriggling as an urgent need to visit there. "If I don't watch that one, we get puddles all over the place," Harriet said, watching the child trot off obediently. "I don't think his mother ever got around to explaining to him what lavatories are for."

"Harriet," Sally said with exaggerated patience. "Will you please concentrate on me for a moment? I want to know what is to happen tonight. Are you coming with us, or aren't you?"

Together, they went into the office, and Harriet sat down at her desk and swung her chair round to look at her friend where she sprawled in the armchair.

"I don't want to," she said. "You know I don't. But what can I do? Paul just won't take no for an answer."

"Then you *are* coming?" Sally said.

"I suppose so. I wish Paul wouldn't nag so —"

"What it is to be Harriet Brett!" Sally said theatrically. "Two men on a string! How do you do it? What have you got that I haven't? Just the same, if a little less of it —" and she looked down at her round shape with a sigh. "How goes things on the Weston front?"

16

Harriet grimaced at the pun, and said "I don't know what you mean —" avoiding Sally's eye as she said it.

"Come off it! You know damned well what I mean! You've been going around with him for nearly two months now. Are you any nearer getting to know him than you were before?"

Harriet sighed. "Not really," she said unwillingly. "We walk a lot and talk a lot, but that's about all." She leaned back in her chair, and stared down the ward absently. "It's odd, you know. I've told him all about myself — about the family, that sort of thing, and he seems interested — asks about them, asks about me — what I like, what I don't like. But somehow we never get around to talking about him. For all I know, he just happened — like Topsy. He never says anything at all about his own background, or where he comes from —"

"Have you asked him — outright, I mean?" Sally said curiously. "I would."

Harriet smiled. "I know you would. If I didn't tell you everything you want to know about my private life you'd only nag me skinny till I did —"

"Why not? If you don't ask, you never know — and I like to know. *Have* you asked him about himself?"

Harriet shook her head.

"He's not that sort of man. I don't deny I've — fished a bit. But he always clams up, and I'm not the sort to persist when someone isn't willing to talk. So there it is —"

"Has he ever kissed you?" Sally asked baldly.

"Sally, really!" Harriet said crossly. "You go too far sometimes —"

"Has he?" Sally ignored the protest.

"No," Harriet said shortly. For a moment, she remembered the way he always seemed not to notice her upturned face whenever he brought her back to the nurses' home, the way her whole body ached to feel his hands over hers when they sat side by side in a threatre or cinema, the way he got out of the car as soon as they got back to the hospital, never once lingering as other men did after a date — as Paul always did.

"I suppose he's all right," Sally said, a question in her voice.

"All right?" Harriet echoed, and stared at Sally, "What do you mean?"

Sally shrugged, embarrassed for once. "You know what I mean. Some men just — never make passes at women."

Harriet reddened with a mixture of embarrassment and anger. "If you are suggesting he's at all gay, you're wrong," she said shortly. "I've been around long enough to recognise a man when I meet one. He's perfectly 'all right' as you put it. I'm sure of that. No — it's something else —"

What she didn't tell Sally about and didn't intend to yet, if she could help it — though she knew quite well that Sally would get it out of her eventually — was the conversation they had had the last time they had been out together. They had been sitting over the remains of dinner at a small restaurant Gregory had taken her to once before, and he had said suddenly, without looking at her, "Harriet — I want to talk to you."

She had looked up from the glass of amber wine she had been twisting between her fingers, and said softly, her heart lifting with a wild hope for a moment, "Yes? What is it, Gregory?"

He had leaned back in his seat, so that his face was hidden in the shadows of the dimly lit restaurant.

"You — do you enjoy these evenings we spend together? The afternoons when we walk around the streets? Or do you just come because you're sorry for me? Think I'm lonely, and that you can help me to be less of a hermit?"

Harriet had smiled then. "Of course I enjoy them, Gregory. I wouldn't come otherwise. I'm not the sort to go in for pity, you know. Not like that. Any pity I've got I use in my job. Outside of that, I live like anyone else — doing what I want to do, because I want to do it. I don't see you as a pitiful object anyway."

"I'm glad of that," he had said gravely. "I'd hate to think you were just — mothering me. I don't like motherly women." He had paused then, and after a moment went on with an oddly painful note in his voice. "I enjoy these times we spend together, too, Harriet. They — they've come to mean a lot to me. Are you a patient woman, Harriet?"

She had stared at him then, surprised by the sudden shift.

"Patient? I don't know. It depends. I can be, I think. If I *must* wait to get what I want, then I *can* wait — is that what you mean?"

He had leaned forward then, so that she could see his face, see the red lamplight glinting on his cheekbones, deepening the fine lines round his mouth.

"I can't explain now — not really. But it's just this. Would you be willing to go on as we are — going out like this, seeing each other whenever we're off duty together, and leave it at that — just for a while? It's a lot to ask, I know. You're a — popular girl, aren't you? I mayn't spend much time in the mess, but I'm there often enough to know that Martin regards you rather highly —"

Harriet reddened. "Paul is — is an old friend," she said a little brusquely. "I've known him a long time."

"Yes — I gathered that. Harriet — would it be asking a lot of you to go on seeing me? And then, in eighteen months' time, perhaps — perhaps we can talk about the future." His voice died away, and for a long moment, Harriet stared at him.

"Eighteen months?" she asked at length. "Eighteen months? I — I don't understand."

"I can't explain — not now," he had said miserably. "I will be able to — then. But not now. Are you patient, Harriet? Can you accept that and understand enough not to ask questions?"

She had sat and looked at him, at the face she had come to love so much, the deep set eyes, the glint of white in his dark hair, and thought confusedly, Wait? What for? For you to love me? Will you ever love me? Are you trying to tell me that you do care for me now? And if you do, why must you wait for so long to "talk of the future"?

He had seemed to interpret her silence as refusal, for he had leaned back, and said in a flat voice, "I'm sorry, Harriet. I had no right to suggest it. It's a lot to ask a woman to take on trust."

20

She had put her hand out impulsively, and said softly, "You had all the right in the world, Gregory. I can't pretend to understand — but that doesn't matter. I —" she picked her words with care. "I enjoy your company a great deal, Gregory. I would be very unhappy if we couldn't see each other as we do. And if you want to go on as we are, that's fine with me."

He had stared at her then, his face lifting into a rare smile. "Thank you, Harriet. Thank you. I — my God, I wish I could explain — but I can't — not yet —"

"Then don't try. If you don't want to talk about anything, you don't have to. I'm not a baby, Gregory. I'm a grown woman — and I hope I'm intelligent enough to accept a situation I can't understand yet in the promise that I will understand it eventually. Gregory —" she had looked down at her hands, loosely clasped on the tablecloth, and with a steady voice that surprised her, she said, "Gregory — you know, don't you? Know I — I care a good deal for you?" She lifted her eyes to look at him. "I'm not good at pretending, Gregory. And there it is."

"I know," he had said in a low voice. "That's why I — why I had to ask you to wait for me. I — I care for you too, Harriet. More than you might suspect. Just give me time, Harriet. Just time."

And that had been all. They had gone back to the hospital in silence, not a strained one, but a silence full of thought on both their parts, though Harriet couldn't even begin to try to imagine just what form Gregory's thinking was taking. He had said goodnight with his usual formality, only saying "thank you" in a low voice before driving back to the main courtyard from the Nurses' Home, leaving Harriet staring after the winking tail lights of his car, her mind whirling.

Even now, two days later, she couldn't assess her own feelings. Part of her was full of relief, relief that this man she loved with all her heart cared for her. But the rest of her mind seethed with questions. Why eighteen months? Why hadn't he made any attempt to kiss her? He must know — she was sure he knew — how much she wanted to feel his touch. And she knew, too, with all the woman in her, that he wanted to hold her close. Why didn't he? Why?

Sally's voice pulled her out of her abstraction.

"Here's Paul," she said hurriedly. "I'm going."

Harriet looked across the ward to the big double doors where Paul Martin's tall figure was standing with a small girl clutching at his white coat. He looked up and saw her at the same moment, and disentangling the child he made his way with an oddly purposeful tread towards the office.

"Don't go, Sally," Harriet said urgently. "Stay —"

"Not on your life, ducky," Sally said. "I'm sick of playing gooseberry to you two. You settle this on your own. 'Bye!" and she slipped out of the office, to stop and say a few words to Paul before disappearing through the doors.

He came in to stand beside the desk, where she immediately busied herself over a chart, trying to present a calm façade.

"Hello, Harriet," he said, putting a hand on her shoulder to pull her round so that she had to look at him.

22

"Hello, Paul," she said with a brightness that rang false even in her own ears.

"Have you come to see that child with the Still's disease? He's doing very well on steroids —"

"No I haven't," he said flatly. "I've come to see you."

"Paul, really, I can't stop now just for social visits. I've far too much to do — the ward's pretty busy —"

"You're always too busy to see me. And you've broken more dates than I care to count. The way you go on, you'd think no one else worked on this ward. You can't be kept late on duty *every* night — and you know damned well you're avoiding me. What is it, Harriet? What have I done?"

She rubbed her face wearily. "I'm sorry, Paul — truly I am. But — I have been busy, really I have."

"You didn't used to be," he said softly. "Not at first. Remember?"

"That was a long time ago, Paul. Things change —" she looked at him miserably. "Please, Paul, don't force me to say hurtful things. I've tried to show you — but you keep persisting —"

"What else can I do?" he said roughly. "I *need* you, Harriet — and all you do is slip away all the time — I can't *get* at you. You hide behind Stephen and Sally whenever we're together — you never give us a chance to be on our own — what's the matter, for Christ's sake? I thought — I thought you cared for me once."

"I thought so too, Paul," Harriet said unhappily. "But I — I was wrong, I suppose. Can't we just — just be friends? Please, Paul — try to understand."

23

He looked at her, his face full of misery. "Friends? Is that the best you can do, Harriet? I love you — you know that, don't you? I want — I want to marry you, Harriet —"

"Don't — please, Paul, don't!" She couldn't bear the misery on his face, the look of a slapped child that filled his eyes.

"It's no use bleating 'Don't' at me," he said, anger suddenly flaring at him. "It's a bit late for that now. At the beginning you weren't like this. If you hadn't been so affectionate then, do you suppose I'd have got myself into this state over you? What do you think I am, for God's sake? A bloody idiot? You can't just act as though you love me one minute and drop me like a piece of garbage the next! Is that all you are — one of those women who like to get a man into a state and then stand back and watch him squirm while you giggle?"

She closed her eyes in sick distress for a moment.

"I suppose I deserved that," she said at length. "But it isn't true, Paul. I don't deny I thought I cared for you at first — but I was wrong. And that's that. I've been trying to avoid this — this sort of scene. I thought if I avoided *you* you'd understand and we could end an episode with — with dignity and still be friends. I was wrong. I should have told you outright."

He thrust his hands deep into the pockets of his white coat and turned to stare down the ward.

"I'm sorry, I shouldn't have said that," he said at last. "I should have known better than to think I could salvage anything out of this by being — unpleasant. I've been trying to persuade myself it wasn't true, I suppose. About you and Weston."

"Weston?" she said awkwardly.

"This is a hospital, remember? You don't suppose you can go around with someone here without everyone knowing about it, do you?"

"I hadn't thought of that," she said slowly. "I'm sorry, Paul. But at least you know now."

"I can't think what you see in him," Paul turned from the window to look at her. "Look, Harriet — this isn't just me being a — a bad loser. But he's an odd bloke — secretive. No one knows anything about him. At his age — well, he's a bit of an oddity. Most men at his stage are married. For all you know he *is* — had you thought of that?"

She stared at him, her chin lifting. "I'm not going to discuss him with you, Paul. It's none of your concern."

"No — I suppose not. The fact that I love you and I'm stupid enough to go on loving you even when you don't want me to gives me no right to be interested in what happens to you," he said bitterly. I'm sorry to be a nuisance."

"Please, Paul — don't be so angry," she said impulsively. "It's — it's very kind of you to be concerned. But this is my affair. And whatever Gregory is or isn't, I — care for him. Please, try to accept that, will you?"

"I've no choice, have I?" He went to the door, and pushed it open. "Forget tonight's date, then, Harriet. Let me break this one for once, hmm? It'll make a change," and he pushed his way out of the ward, ignoring the children who looked up at him in surprise, missing the sweets he usually carried in his pockets for them.

She stood and stared after him, sick with misery, yet at the same time oddly relieved that the whole thing had happened. At least he knew now, at least he would stop following her around, forcing her to think up ever more excuses for not going out with him. But —

A nurse put her head round the office door.

"The lunch trolley is up, Sister," she said. "Are you ready to serve them?"

"Mmm? Oh, yes. I'm just coming —"

She served the children's meals abstractedly, filling plates with minced beef and vegetables, making sure that all the toddlers were fed, checking the special diets automatically. And all the time, Paul's voice rang over and over in her mind.

"Most men at his stage are married. For all you know he *is* — had you thought of that?"

And it was this that surprised her. Because she hadn't. In all the long hours she had spent thinking about Gregory, about his need for time, his promise that after eighteen months they could "talk about the future" it had never occurred to her that he might be married, that it might be this that stood between them.

She sent the nurses to their own lunch, and settled the children in their cots for their afternoon naps, pulling blinds so that the thin winter sunshine was blotted out, walking round the ward softly, promising the unhappy ones that their mothers would soon be coming to visit them, wiping lunch-smeared faces clean, giving chocolate to those who could have it. And all the time, her thoughts whirled with a sick persistence. Why? Was he married? Wasn't he?

For the rest of that long afternoon, as she went through the usual routine that was the day's work she thought about it. And at half past six, when she went off duty for the evening, she had at last come to a decision. She would ask him. He had asked for patience, but she would ask him for this one explanation. She had to know.

CHAPTER
THREE

There was a bitter wind blowing, whipping her apron high, tugging at her cap, as she hurried across the courtyard through the early darkness of the winter evening. But cold as it was, she paused for a moment at the gate that opened on to the Nurses Home path, and looked back across the wide courtyard at the hospital.

The main ward block loomed blackly into the wintry sky, pierced at regular intervals with the oblong yellow patches that were the ward windows. She could see the shapes of nurses flitting past each window as they hurried round the wards, preparing the patients for supper, see high on the fifth floor the dimmer red oblongs that were the windows of her own ward, where the children were already asleep. There was a faint white patch out on the balcony, and automatically she thought — Nurse Jenkins — she's forgotten to bring those bits of washing in again. It's no wonder we lose linen. Those nightgowns'll blow away any minute. I'll give her a rocket in the morning —

It's odd, she thought. This place is full of misery for so many people. Everything about it is alarming. The huge impersonal mass of it, the faint smell of antiseptic and anaesthetics that could be recognised even out here, in the windy courtyard. Visitors, patients — they can't get away from the place quickly enough. But for me, this is home, this is security. For a brief moment, she let her mind run off into fantasy, imagining herself working here for the rest of her life, giving all of herself to the illnesses of other people, gaining peace of mind and security while she did it. Wouldn't that be better — infinitely better — than this aching yearning inside her, this longing for one person's presence, this need for one man's touch? She felt as though she were poised on the edge of a huge pool of water. She could choose — still choose, choose whether to turn back from the edge to the safety of dry land that stood behind, or whether to take a big breath and leap into the water in front of her, the water that symbolised in her fantasy the relationship she was trying to build with Gregory, the relationship that she was trying to end with Paul.

And then, her intellect took over, and with a wry grin in the darkness she remembered her psychology lectures. Water, in dreams and fantasies — water was the recognised symbol of sex. The psychologists are right, she told herself. Why else would I see myself as standing on the edge of a pool, why else do I see my situation as that of a swimmer battling against huge waves, being buffeted by the sheer weight of blue water? I wish I were less of a woman, that I didn't have this need for Gregory. But there was no escaping it. She had already jumped into her pool, was already committed to building her future with Gregory, and no matter how much she wanted to turn back, avoid the uncertainty that the future seemed to hold, she could not. She loved him.

There was nothing else to be done but go on loving him.

Shivering a little, she turned and hurried on. I'll phone him, she thought, see if he's off duty tonight, and suggest we go out for a drink somewhere. And then I'll ask him. I must. If he is married, I must know. Quite what she would do if he admitted he was, she didn't allow herself to consider. That hazard must be dealt with as it arose. No amount of thought now could guide her. As she got to the Home, and stood in the brightly lit hall, blinking a little as she shook the creases out of her apron, the receptionist who sat all day in the little cubby hole that held the small Home switchboard put her head out of the door, and called, "Sister Brett!"

"Letter for me?" Harriet asked. There should be a letter from Sybil, her sister. She hadn't written for a week or more, though Harriet had learned to accept her sister's spasmodic letters as normal; a busy Vicar's wife, with three small children of her own, a couple of foster children, as well as all the parish work to do and a huge rambling house to look after, had little time for the luxury of letter writing.

"Yes, Sister." The receptionist smirked at her with elephantine roguishness. "A special one — internal mail, you could call it. Brought it himself, he did. It's here —" She fumbled beneath the cluttered shelf in front of the switchboard, and brought out a small parcel, wrapped in white tissue paper, with a square white envelope stuck to it with a piece of transparent sticky tape.

Surprised, Harriet took it. The envelope had "Sister Brett" written on it in a strong slanting handwriting, and for a moment she stared at it in mystification.

The receptionist giggled, and said again, "Brought it in himself he did. Isn't that nice?"

"Who brought it?" Harriet asked stupidly.

"Why, that nice looking doctor did — I don't know his name, mind you — I don't get to see the doctors very often. Know their voices on the 'phone, like, but not their faces. Very distinguished he looks, doesn't he? I like a man as *looks* like a man myself. And that grey in his hair — very distinguished looking, isn't it, Sister?"

"Yes —" Harriet said absently, "Very distinguished. Thank you, Miss Chester —"

She took the parcel and the letter up to her room to open them; much to the disappointment of Miss Chester, who liked to share in as much of the nursing staff's life as she could. Even watching someone open a letter gave her a vicarious thrill, a sense of sharing in a busy life, for her own was notable only for its lack of incident.

Harriet sat on the edge of her bed, her cape in a heap on the floor at her feet, and put the little white parcel down beside her. Slowly, she pulled her cap off, and ran her fingers through her hair, staring at the writing on the envelope like a woman in a trance.

Why on earth should he write to me? Has he had second thoughts? Is he regretting saying what he did — the promise of "talk about the future" in eighteen months time? I won't open it — panic rose in her — I won't.

But she shook her head in impatience at her own stupidity, and pulling her scissors from her belt, slit the thick white envelope.

"My dear Harriet" — the strong slanting writing began — "you will no doubt think me quite absurd to be writing to you in this way when I am so near to you, when I could come to the ward to talk to you, could arrange for us to go out somewhere where we could talk face to face. But I find it a great deal easier to talk to you like this, with a pen and paper. I've lost the habit — if I ever had it, which I begin to doubt — of being able to say all I would like to say in the usual way. So, a letter.

"I want to thank you, Harriet, for your promise of patience, your calm acceptance of what must seem to you an unpleasant secretiveness on my part. I have learned to care a great deal for your opinion of me — long before that scalded child gave me an opportunity to take you out of the hospital somewhere, to have your company away from a ward full of children and nurses, I wanted to do just that. And I was right in what I had first seen in you. You have a serenity, an adult maturity of understanding that I would not have expected in someone as young as you are. I'm thirty-eight, you know — and you're just twenty-five. But even though I have thirteen years on you, you make me feel that in some ways you are infinitely older than I am with that maturity that is so wonderful a part of you.

"It is that maturity in you that makes me so happy now. I know I need not fear what I would certainly have to fear in any other woman — a probing, a nagging if you like, an inability to accept without questions. Because I could not bear to be questioned. Believe me, if I could explain to you now why I cannot say to you all that I would like to say, why I cannot yet give you all I would like to give you, I would. But with you, I need not be afraid, need I? Thank you for that, Harriet.

"But even if I cannot yet give what I want to give, I can offer you one concrete object as a small token of my appreciation and esteem. Please accept it.

"And please, don't let us talk of this letter when we meet to go to the theatre next Friday. I'm so very bad at talking. Gregory."

She let the letter drop onto her lap, and stared out of her window at the few stars that shone steadily in the dark panes, at her reflection, a little twisted by the distortion in the glass, and felt again that odd mixture of joy and frustration that she was coming to recognise as an inevitable part of her feeling for Gregory.

So that's that. I can't ask him now. How could I? Not now. For a moment she hated Paul, Paul whose hurt anger had made him suggest that Gregory was a married man, that he was too secretive to be otherwise. Until Paul had said so, it had never occurred to her that this might be the case. But then her anger subsided, for she realised quite well that the same thought would have come to her eventually, even if Paul had never said anything.

Her hand slid off her lap, and with a start, she looked down at the little parcel that it had touched. Slowly, she picked it up, and began to peel off the layers of tissue paper.

It was a tiny piece of French porcelain, a model of a girl sitting on a bench, her lap full of flowers. It was barely three inches high, yet every detail of the tiny face was perfect, each petal of every flower breathtakingly beautiful in its minute detail. The colour was exquisite, the girl's dress falling to her delicate feet in folds of cerulean blue, the flowers in tints of pale lemon and pink, with shimmering green leaves. And the girl herself had hair that was the colour of sherry, a soft amber tinted brown, each carefully modelled strand of hair curling with a reality that made it look as though it could be curled round a finger, if there were a finger small enough to do it. Her eyes, eyes that looked into the distance with a melancholy that seemed to transmit itself to the beholder, were the same colour, with minute flecks of lighter amber in them.

Harriet stared at the lovely thing, and then, without stopping to think, took it across the room to her dressing table. She switched on the light in front of the mirror, and bent to look into the glass, holding the little figure against her face. The hair was exactly the same colour as her own, the eyes that looked so remotely into the mirror seemed to sparkle a little, seemed to recognise the same amber flecks in the depths of Harriet's own eyes.

She put it down in front of the light, and sank slowly into the chair in front of the dressing table. The little figure threw its shadow in front of itself, the girl's face seeming to droop sadly in the flood of light above it, the tiny mouth looking as though it would tremble into life at any moment.

And then, Harriet wept, drooping her head into her hands and giving herself up to an agony of sobbing that seemed as though it would shake her to pieces.

So lost was she in her weeping, so isolated in her distress, she didn't hear the door open behind her, didn't realise that she wasn't alone until she felt Sally's hands on her shoulders.

"Harriet — Harriet, honey, what is it? What's the matter? Is something wrong at home? What is it, love?" Sally dropped to her knees beside Harriet, and pulled her round till she was weeping against her friend's shoulder, patting the heaving back in an effort to stop the tearing gulping sobs.

Gradually, Harriet regained control of herself, managed to sit up again, groping for a handkerchief to mop at her red eyes.

"I'm sorry, Sally — I didn't mean — I'm sorry —" she said huskily, scrubbing at her face, blowing her nose, trying to control the painful breathing that still tugged unevenly at her chest.

Sally, practical as always, thrust her hand into her pocket, and pulled out a crumpled pack of cigarettes. Gently, she put one between Harriet's shaking lips, and lit it.

"I'll be right back," she said crisply, and went purposefully from the room to return a few seconds later with a toothglass in her hand.

"Here you are, lovey. Whisky," she said. "I keep it for Stephen, but he can spare this one."

Harriet took it, and coughed a little as the raw spirit pulled at her throat, then relaxed slowly as the warmth of it began to spread through her chilled body.

Sally sat down on the bed, and looked at Harriet where she slumped in the dressing table chair.

"Now, lovey. Tell me what's upset you." Then, as Harriet began to shake her head, she said, a little roughly, "You'd be much better if you did — I'm not just prying, Harriet, believe me, but talking about whatever it is'll help. Come on, now."

Harriet stubbed out the cigarette and stood up, going to stand at the window, to stare out at the winter darkness, the deep shadows under the trees of the Nurses' Home garden, breathing deeply of the rich wet smell of rotting leaves that came up through the slightly opened window.

"It's all such a mess, Sally," she said at length, her voice heavy with reaction. "Such a mess."

"Gregory? Or Paul?" Sally asked from behind her.

"Both, I suppose." Almost in surprise, Harriet realised that her storm of tears owed as much to her distress at the scene with Paul that morning as to her feeling about Gregory. "He — Paul — we had an argument, if you can call it that, this morning. But he knows now. I won't be going out with him any more — and he won't ask me to again either."

She turned to look at Sally then, came to sit beside her.

"I want it that way, believe me, Sal. But — well, it's been a long time, hasn't it? And even if I don't love him now, I did once — a little. It hurts when things die, even if you want them to. And I hate making Paul so miserable. He's a — a bit like a child, in some ways. I feel as though I've abandoned him. Or does that sound arrogant? I don't know —"

"No, you aren't being arrogant, Harriet. He does need you, I think. And he is a bit — immature, I suppose. He needs people all the time — needs their admiration to bolster himself in his own estimation," Sally said. "But that immaturity'll be his salvation, in a way. He'll —

36

what's the word? — he'll rationalise his way out of this. Does he know about Gregory?"

Harriet nodded.

"It's just as well," Sally went on. "I mean, he'll be less hurt, in a way. It would have been much worse for him if you'd rejected him just because you found you didn't care for him. This way, he'll see himself as a sort of — honourable loser. Do you know what I mean?"

Harriet managed a smile, and put her hand out to touch Sally's. "Bless you, Sal. You make me mad sometimes, but you know how to say the sort of things that'll help me when I need help. I think you're probably right. Paul will get over this. I'm not the end of his world, and I needn't persuade myself that I am. It's a comfort."

"But it wasn't only Paul you were crying about, was it?" Sally said shrewdly. "What else, Harriet?"

And Harriet, lost as she was in the conflicting state of her feelings about Gregory, told her. About his need for time, his request for patience on her part, the letter, the gift of the porcelain girl and her lapful of flowers.

"What can I do, Sally?" she asked piteously. "What can I do? I love him — it's as though I never felt anything in my life before I felt this. He's everything to me — if he didn't exist, I think I wouldn't — not properly. I'd just be a shell without this feeling. I'm lost, Sal — lost," and for a moment, tears rose in her again, threatening to swamp her in a luxury of bitter weeping.

Sally put a strong warm hand on Harriet's cold one, and said with brisk practicality. "Then you'll have to learn to live *with* it, Harriet. I can't pretend to understand properly — I guess I'm just not made for the grand passion. But you — you're different. All you can do is hold on to things as they are. If he loves you — and you think he does —"

For a moment Harriet stopped to think, and then relaxed. She didn't need to think.

"Yes," she said softly. "He loves me. I know that, if I know nothing else. He hasn't said so in so many words, but he loves me. It's odd, really. I know it as surely as I know I love him —"

"Well, then, it's all right, isn't it? People like me and Stephen — well, if things don't pan out for us, it's because we're not made as people like you and Gregory are. But they'll come right for you, Harriet. They'll have to, won't they? God knows how, but it'll *have* to come right. If he's anything like you are — and I suppose he must be, or you wouldn't love him as you do — then it's inevitable. Whatever happens in between, somehow it'll come right." Sally grinned a little shyly. "I'm not explaining this well, Harriet, I suppose. It's just something I feel. Like algebra."

Diverted for a moment, Harriet stared at her.

"You know — you can't understand exactly, you struggle with all those ghastly figures and a's and b's and x's and y's, and you think none of it can possibly make sense — but all the time you know it does, really. That there's an answer there somewhere, a logical obvious answer if only you can find it." Sally groped a little. "That's how it is with you. You're lost in a mess of numbers and letters, and you can't see the way out. But it's there — somehow, it *is* there —"

And suddenly, Harriet knew she was right. No matter what misery she felt now, no matter what happened, somehow it would one day be right. She and Gregory. Together, one day, they would find the obvious logical perfect answer to everything they had ever needed.

CHAPTER
FOUR

Harriet was more than usually grateful for Christmas this year. As she sat at breakfast the next morning, a little abstracted over her coffee and toast, the voices of the other Sisters, discussing with varying degrees of anticipation the preparations they would be making for the holiday in their own wards, she pulled her thoughts away from her private problems, and forced herself to think about what would be happening on the children's ward. Sally grinned at her approvingly as Harriet turned to the Sister from the Maternity block and asked her whether she could share her Crib fittings this year. The Sister from the Maternity block immediately assured Harriet that she hadn't as much as an Ox or an Ass to spare, so many pieces of her Crib had been broken the year before, and Sally laughed at Harriet's chagrined face as the other Sister swept huffily from the dining room.

"Attagirl!" she said softly. "Much better for you to get peeved with old Misery-Chops than think about Gregory or Paul. I must say — I'm damned grateful I'm on Theatres come Christmas. We may have a hell of a life all the year round, but at least we don't have to spend hours filling stockings and decorating wards —"

"Oh, I don't know," Harriet said, ignoring the reference to her problems with the men in her life. "It wouldn't be Christmas for me if I didn't have a ward full of children to think about — I enjoy the rush — and the stockings are fun. And since you aren't busy yourself, you can come and help me with them. I'll have thirty to fill, and that means hours of shopping. I'll see how much money the office have for me to spend this year, and let you know when we're going to get the stuff — and you aren't getting out of helping, I promise you —"

"Why can't I keep my big mouth shut?" Sally groaned. "I swear I'll be too busy —"

"Nuts!" said Harriet, firmly. "You can come shopping with me — and if you're good, I might even let you wrap the sweets for the stockings. You'll love that — you can eat yourself sick on jelly babies —"

The next three weeks went by in a rush of normal ward work complicated by Christmas preparations. Each afternoon, the children who were well enough collected around the big table in the middle of the ward, dressing gown sleeves rolled up, piles of coloured strips of paper in front of them, a glue pot apiece and a brush clutched in each small hand, to manufacture strings of rather grubby and wobbly paper chains. Harriet loved these afternoons. The children were so happy, so absorbed in their paper work, and she would look at the small concentrating faces shining under the big lights, pink tongues held between teeth, happy to see them so involved. It's a wonderful thing to be so young, she would think sometimes, so utterly wrapped up in the present. When you are five, tomorrow has little meaning

— only today — this very minute — counts, and Harriet watched the children, and learned to be like them, thinking only of the moment and its work, thinking nothing about tomorrow and its problems.

The day before Christmas Eve, she and her nurses set to work to decorate the ward. The children were full of excitement, squealing joyfully as the nurses dragged the big boxes of prepared paper chains and tree trimmings into the ward, jumping excitedly on their beds and cots as Harriet began to blow up balloons. For the children Christmas had already begun, and Harriet laughed a little ruefully as she listened to the noise they made, the shrieks of joy whenever a balloon, blown too enthusiastically, burst loudly into shreds of coloured rubber.

"They'll all need tranquillisers tonight," she told her staff nurse above the hubbub. "At this rate, they'll all be dead from excitement before tomorrow —"

But she caught their excitement, too, as several of the doctors arrived in the ward to join in the fun of decorating. However busy the rest of the hospital was, most of the staff tried to come to the children's ward for a while to help — it was the warmest and happiest place in the building at Christmas. In the other wards, patients tended to be depressed and miserable, sad to be spending Christmas in hospital instead of at home, but here, the children were just plain happy, even the homesick ones joining in the laughter and the oohs and ahs of delight as each string of coloured paper snaked across the ward.

By six o'clock, the decorating was finished. Bright loops of paper chains covering the ceiling, criss-crossing round the lights in a fretwork of red and blue and yellow and green, balloons hung in fat bunches over each bed, and the huge Christmas Tree in the middle of the ward shimmered with tinsel and the fairy lights, strings of fluffy white popcorn gleaming gently against the deep green of the branches, translucent baubles swaying and turning in every breath of a draught that moved across the big room. Harriet turned the main lights off when the tree was finished, and stood at the end of the ward looking at the children perched on their beds as they stared at the tree with flushed faces, eyes sparkling in the reflection of light from the strings of winking fairy bulbs, gazing up at the big twinkling star that Harriet had fixed firmly to the topmost branch.

The ward slid into a breathless silence as the children stared, open-mouthed and absorbed, and the adults stood in the shadows and looked sympathetically at them. Harriet's heart twisted sharply with pity as she looked at them, sad that their very youth was so transient. Soon, very soon, she thought sombrely, they'll grow up and the world won't be a sparkling place any more, a place of gay Christmas trees and tinsel and balloons. And then she shook herself impatiently and began to tuck the children in for the night, quietly shooing out the doctors and nurses from other wards, so that the children could be soothed into a restful state of mind, ready for sleep.

The following day was full of activity, as Harriet and her nurses tried to fit the business of stocking filling into the day's routine. The children were all excited, as parents brought mysterious parcels to stack on each bedside locker, as more parcels piled up under the Tree, ready to be distributed next day by Santa Claus. There was an hilarious half hour for the nurses in the kitchen when Dr Bennett, the senior consultant, came to be fitted for the Santa Claus suit, and stood awkward and self conscious as Harriet draped the red suit round his lean frame, and showed him how to hook the fluffy white beard over his ears.

It was long past six when the stockings were ready to be distributed, lying in piles on the floor of Harriet's office, and then Harriet and the nurses set about the solemn ritual of hanging empty stockings on each bed and cot. Harriet was nothing if not thorough, and she had collected thirty empty stockings, huge white operating ones, to be hung on each bed, as well as preparing thirty full of toys and sweets and fruit.

She went from bed to bed, cot to cot, tucking each small body under the covers, carefully helping each child hook his white stocking on the end of his bed, promising them all that Santa Claus would come. One small boy, a five year old wearing a big bandage over the head injury he had got in a traffic accident asked her anxiously how Santa Claus would know where he was?

"Last year, I was at home," he explained worriedly. "An' he knows where I live. I haven't told him I'm here now — how will he know?"

"I 'phoned him," Harriet assured him gravely. "This morning. I 'phoned him specially, to tell him who was here this year, and he said that would be all right —"

"Oh —" the little boy thought for a minute, "Well, that's all right then. Mummy said he's bringing a puppy this year, you see, so it's important. It'd be awful if he took the puppy and put him in the wrong stocking, wouldn't it?" and he snuggled happily down under the covers, peering trustfully up at Harriet.

"Ah — well, now, the puppy," Harriet said, thinking fast. "He did mention that — and asked me to give you a message. He said would you mind if he sent the puppy to your house? He's got some other things to bring for your stocking here, but he thought it would be better if he took the puppy to your house — he's a shy puppy, you see, and Santa Claus thought he might be a bit upset with all these people around —"

The little boy bit his lip, and tears brimmed in his eyes for a moment, and hurriedly, Harriet said. "I'll tell you what. I'll 'phone your Mummy and Daddy, and ask them to bring the puppy to see you tomorrow — will that be all right? Then you'll know he's arrived safely."

The little boy sighed, and then nodded. "I s'pose so. Poor old puppy — do you think he'll mind my bandage when he sees it?"

"Not a bit," Harriet assured him, tucking the bedclothes round the slender neck. "You'll see —"

And as soon as she had finished her round of all the children, she spent ten minutes on the 'phone explaining to the little boy's parents what she had promised their son, and they assured her gratefully that the puppy had indeed been bought, and would be brought to the hospital the next afternoon.

She went off duty at eight, weary, but happy, too involved with the preparations for the next day to think much of anything at all. Indeed, she was so absorbed, that when a hand fell on her shoulder as she hurried along the lower corridor towards the nurses' home, where the staff were collecting to set off on their carol singing tour of the wards, she nearly jumped out of her skin.

"Merry Christmas, Harriet."

It was Gregory, and she whirled to look up at him, to feel the familiar lurch of pleasure at the sight of his thin face and tired eyes, the drumming of her pulses in her ears at the nearness of him.

"Merry — merry Christmas, Gregory," she said, smiling up at him.

"I've bought a present for you. I was going to put it under the tree in the ward, but — well, I'd like to give it to you now," and he pushed a small parcel into her hand, and stood smiling a little diffidently at her.

She looked up at him in the dimly lit corridor, and said breathlessly, "You — you shouldn't — really —"

"Why not? I want to. I — I haven't many people to give presents to. Let me have the pleasure of giving one to you —"

And Harriet laughed a little shyly. "You — you'll find a parcel under the tree in the doctors' common room," she said softly. "I hope you'll like it —"

Three of the other Sisters came bustling along the corridor towards them. "Come on, Brett!" One of them called, pulling at her arm as they went by. "You'll be late for the carols —" And Harriet let herself be hurried away, smiling back to Gregory over her shoulder as she went, clutching her little parcel under her cape.

All through the carol singing, as the little procession of nurses wound its way through the hospital's wards and corridors, their capes turned inside out to show the bright red linings, she could feel the weight of the parcel in her pocket bumping softly against her leg as she walked. The wards were dimly lit, only the tree in the middle of each one sparkling with its fairy lights, as the nurses padded softly past each bed, their voices high and clear as they sang the familiar melodies. And, as every year, Harriet felt sympathetic tears pricking her own eyes as she saw women lying against the white pillows wipe tears from their cheeks as they listened, saw men sniff loudly and bury their chins in their pyjama jackets so that the nurses wouldn't see the bright gleam of tears in their eyes. Only on the maternity ward, where they sang the traditional "Unto us a son is born" did the sense of sadness, of the loneliness of people forced to be ill in hospital instead of happily at home, leave her. They stood in the middle of the maternity ward, singing lustily, smiling a little when one or two of the babies, lying in cots next to their mothers' beds, joined in with thin wails, crumpled fists waving furiously as they cried.

And later, when the carolling was finished, and Harriet returned to her own ward, to creep softly from bed to bed, replacing the limp empty stockings with bulging ones, she felt again the sense of certainty that somehow, no matter what, all would come out well for her in the end. She felt, obscurely, that whatever happened with Gregory and Paul, however sad she may be in the future because of Gregory, some things would always be the same, some sources of happiness and contentment would always remain to her. There would always be work, always be Christmas, and in

47

these things, there was a sort of happiness to be found. "Even if I never do find a life with Gregory," she told herself as she walked across the courtyard towards the nurses' home, and the traditional sherry party in the Sisters' sitting room, "There will always be something to enjoy."

And when, last thing that night, before she went to bed, she opened her parcel from Gregory, to find another tiny porcelain figure, this time of a dark haired boy leaning over a stile, a cap on the back of his curly head, his tiny legs crossed nonchalantly, his brown eyes looking cheerfully out at the world, she smiled. There were no tears in her this time, no feeling of misery as she looked at the pair of little figures where she set them on her dressing table. For there were two of them; and despising herself a little for her own lapse into superstition, she saw them as a happy omen.

CHAPTER
FIVE

Christmas Day at the Royal followed its time-honuored pattern. Those adult patients who were well enough came in their pyjamas and dressing gowns to the children's ward to watch the excited opening of stockings; nurses snatched minutes from their own wards to trail happily round the hospital admiring the decorations other nurses had put up; the Theatres were full of hilarious doctors stuffing themselves with mince pies and coffee long before ten o'clock; the local Mayor and various dignitaries came to make their usual pompous tour of the wards, and in the kitchens, cooks and dieticians sweated hectically over the dozens of colossal turkeys and plum puddings, working against the clock to have the patients' Christmas dinner ready by noon.

Harriet, trying against all odds to get the usual dressings and treatments done on the children's ward, in a welter of paper wrappings, dealt with those children who managed to eat themselves sick soon after breakfast, and turned a blind eye to those of her nurses who left the ward more often than they should have done on visits to other wards. Christmas Day was one day when a Sister expected to carry the main burden of the ward work, and she didn't really mind having to work so hard — this was one of the nicest parts of being a children's ward sister, and she was happy.

At three o'clock, when the parents filled the ward, and as many of the staff as could had arrived to watch the fun, Dr Bennett, sweating uncomfortably in his red suit, jumped through the fire escape door with many loud "Ho-Ho's!" and a deep "Hello Children!" to distribute the presents from the tree, accompanied as usual by the brawniest medical student who could be found, tastefully dressed in a fairy costume from beneath which hairy legs adorned with football socks and boots capered cheerfully from bed to bed, hugging the children, and kissing every nurse he could catch. Harriet, in her place beside the tree, ready to hand the parcels to Dr Bennett, was just about to begin the job, when the 'phone made itself heard, ringing shrilly above the shrieks of the children, and the giggles of nurses busy dodging the enthusiastic attentions of the fairy. The Staff nurse answered it, and came picking her way through the crowd to whisper in Harriet's ear.

"There's a child with virus pneumonia on her way up, Sister. Dr Weston's bringing her —" and with a sigh, Harriet relinquished her place beside the tree to her staff nurse, and hurried out to a cubicle to prepare for the admission. She always hoped nothing of this sort would happen on Christmas Day, but all too often, it did. Illness was no respecter of occasions.

As she finished opening the cot, setting the electric blanket to warm the sheets, Gregory appeared at the door

50

of the cubicle, a small child held in his arms, an anxious man behind him.

"Acute virus pneumonia," he said shortly, carefully laying the child into the cot. She was very small — barely a year old, and her face, an olive skinned pointed one, with the liquid brown eyes and curling black eyelashes of the Greek Cypriot, was waxy, with tinges of blue round the pinched nostrils, which flared with each struggling inhalation as the child fought to breathe. Her curly black hair was sticking in tendrils to her broad forehead, and she whimpered miserably, struggling weakly against Harriet's gentle hands, as she began to take her clothes off, putting a small gown on the narrow olive-brown body.

"She'll need oxygen —" Gregory was saying, "and some antibiotic — can you get a tent up while I fix a jab for her?"

Harriet nodded, and with rapid movements, pulled an oxygen cylinder towards the bed. Gregory disappeared towards the sterilising room, while carefully, Harriet fixed the small mask from the cylinder over the child's face, and turned to the man hovering anxiously beside the cot.

"You are her father?"

"Huh? Father — yes, father — speak — no English —" the man said, crouching beside the cot to peer with frightened eyes at the small girl tossing a little on the white pillows. "Anna — my Anna — you make well?"

"We'll try —" Harriet said gently. "Please — hold this. I must get a tent up —" and carefully, she put the man's hand on the mask, showing him how to hold it in place, before hurrying to fetch the big polythene oxygen tent, the ice and spare cylinder that would be needed to surround the child with the oxygen she needed so desperately.

She had the tent up round the cot before Gregory returned with an injection ready on a tray, and together, with their arms carefully pushed through the special apertures at the side of the tent, they thrust the fine needle into the small buttock, and as the child squirmed feebly and whimpered, sent the plunger into the barrel, to fill the blood stream with a million units of penicillin.

Beyond the glass-walled cubicle, Harriet could hear the shouts and laughter of the children, the deep voice of Dr Bennett calling names, the squeals of joy as the beefy fairy capered from bed to bed, bringing each child to Santa Claus to get his parcels. Above the tent, inside which small Anna lay breathing agonisingly quickly and shallowly, a bunch of balloons swung with incongruous gaiety, and the head of the silent father, now hovering with piteous anxiety against the wall, was outlined with a loop of gaudy paper chains.

Gregory and Harriet stood silently, looking down on the child in the tent, at the half closed eyes beneath which a rim of blue-white could be seen, making her look sickeningly like a half-dead creature — as indeed she was. And as they watched, her face seemed to get bluer, her neck stretched backwards in an agonising effort to breathe, and her mouth opened in a grimace of pain.

Swiftly, Gregory thrust a hand through the tent to feel for her pulse, as the child suddenly lay quite still, not breathing at all.

"She's in collapse —" he said, and pushed the tent back with impatient fingers.

"Start artificial respiration," he said shortly. "She'll need a direct heart stimulant — where're the other nurses? We'll need help —"

"They're in the ward with Santa Claus —" Harriet said, as she began a rhythmic movement of her hands on the child's thin chest, trying to inflate the small lungs again.

"Bloody Christmas —" Gregory said with a flare of anger, "I'll get someone —"

As he turned to hurry from the cubicle, the medical student appeared at the door, to peer round it with elephantine coyness, "I'm looking for Sister Brett!" he chirped, in a falsetto voice. "Santa Clause wants Sister Brett —" and then, as he saw the tableau of now weeping father, angry Gregory, and desperately working Harriet, he dropped his voice and said quickly, "Need any help?"

"Yes," Gregory said roughly, "Take over here, while we get a heart jab organised — jump to it, man!"

The medical student pulled his frizzy blonde wig from his head, and ran over to the cot, to take Harriet's place at artificial respiration, and she moved away gratefully, already feeling the strain in her shoulders and back from the even movements she had been making. Still the child didn't breathe alone, and the medical student, his frilly tu-tu spread absurdly over the sheets, his face, under its comic plastering of make-up, stern and worried, moved his heavy shoulders gently as he tried to pump air into the still body.

Harriet's fingers shook as she prepared the special syringe in the sterilising room, fixing the long needle in place on the barrel, handing it to Gregory to draw up the colourless stimulant from the small ampoule he had brought from the poison cupboard. "Don't let her die — don't let her die," she prayed silently, as together they hurried back to the cubicle. "Don't let her die —"

Gregory pushed the medical student away from the cot side, as Harriet quickly replaced the mask from the single oxygen cylinder over the blue face, and then held the shoulders straight for Gregory.

With an unusual tact for a medical student the boy in the tu-tu put a friendly arm across the shoulders of the man standing weeping helplessly against the wall, and tried to lead him out, but the man refused to go, holding on to the cot head with one desperate hand, watching Gregory's fingers as he ran his fingertips over the framework of ribs, seeking the place to make the heart injection.

They all held their breath, as they watched him, cocooned in a brilliantly lit glass cubicle while the sounds of singing of "Jingle Bells" came discordantly from the ward beyond, and the glass walls rattled slightly as some of the children in the ward began to bounce on the floor in a dance.

The syringe barrel flashed a little as Gregory found the spot he was seeking, and eased the long needle through the fine skin, deep into the chest. Slowly, his eyes never leaving the child's face, he pushed the plunger home, while Harriet held the bird-frail wrist seeking eagerly for the leaping of a pulse.

But it made no difference, Gregory withdrew his needle, and they stayed very still, watching the tiny body with all their will for her to live in their eyes. But she didn't move, her eyes still half open above the dark green rubber of the mask, the oxygen hissing gently, the respiration bag on the cylinder limp and still.

Gregory moved at last, and leaned forward to take the mask from the little face with steady fingers. He pulled his stethoscope from his pocket, and began to move the bell across the still chest, his eyes abstracted as he listened for signs of life. Then he pulled the earpieces away from his head and stood up.

"I'm sorry," he said to the man, with a brusqueness born of distress. "Sorry. Nothing we can do. We did our best. I'm sorry."

The man stared at him with uncomprehending eyes, as Harriet and the medical student stood in helpless pity. "My Anna?" he said huskily. "You make her well? My Anna? She well soon?"

Harriet moved, walked round the cot to put her hands on his shoulders.

"I'm sorry," she said softly. "So sorry, my dear. But she is dead. We did all we could —"

"No! No —" The man pulled away from her, his eyes blazing with sudden anger. "No —" and he bent to the bed, to pick up the frail body, clutching her close, shaking her, shouting at her in Greek as he tried to make her move, breathe again.

Gregory, with a sudden angry shrug, turned away from him, going to the door.

55

"We aren't God, man — we aren't God!" he said, his voice loud and harsh. "We did all we could — all we could — for Christ's sake —" And then, he came back, his eyes deep and shadowed in his face, to take the dead child from her weeping father.

"Come," he said, laying the child down again on the cot, leaving Harriet to gently pull a sheet up across her small still face. "Come —" And he led the man from the cubicle.

Harriet watched them walk through the ward, past the children and laughing parents, all of whom seemed unaware of any crisis going on, saw the man stumble as the little boy with the bandaged head chased his frisking puppy across the ward, saw them go into her office. There was some brandy there, and she could see Gregory pour a drink out for the man who slumped in the chair and stared out at the noisy ward with blank eyes.

The medical student said with a rough voice that barely disguised the tears that were hovering very near the surface. "Why? Why do kids have to die? Bad enough when old men do — but why kids? I'll never do paediatrics when I qualify — so help me God, I won't —"

Harriet, with a steady movement that belied her own distress began to pull the curtains around the glass walls, ready for the last task of preparing the child to be removed to the mortuary.

"That's stupid," she said huskily. "Stupid. Of course we all feel like that when a child dies — it's tragic waste, bitterly hurtful. But not so long ago, a death like this was commonplace. Children died of pneumonia all the time.

56

But because people who were distressed by their deaths went on caring about children, trying to find ways to stop such deaths, tragedies like this are rare now. That's why it hurts more, in a way. When it was common, doctors — people — everyone really, even parents, took it for granted — it was one of those things. When it happens now, we feel — lost, diminished. If you are really upset as you seem, then you *will* go on to do paediatrics. There's more to caring about children than providing fun —" she looked into the ward again before drawing the last curtain, at the happy faces, the laughing parents, the warm gay busy safety of it all, and with a crisp rattle of curtain rings, shut the sight out, and turned back to the boy standing in ridiculous finery behind her. "And do you know what you're going to do now?" she said to him, putting a hand over one of his cold ones. "You're going to put that absurd wig on again, and you are going to go out into that ward and giggle and caper for all you're worth. Those children and parents there — they don't have to be punished because of your sense of inadequacy, because one child slipped through our fingers. We aren't God — Dr Weston was right — we aren't, and we have no right to make others suffer because we don't always manage to be like gods, and save lives. So go and make those children laugh — go on, now."

He stared at her, his face angry for a moment, as though he would argue. Then he managed a small grin, and nodded, reaching for his frizzy wig to thrust it over his own crew cut head.

"OK, Sister. Thanks a lot," he said, and went. She followed him, and watched as he took a deep breath before leaping into the ward with a squeal, sending the children into renewed gales of mocking laughter.

And then, she too, pulling her stiff face into a semblance of a smile, followed him out, to make her way through the ward to the kitchen, to see that the children's special Christmas Tea was ready.

As she passed the office, Gregory and the man came out, Gregory's arm over his shoulders, and she took his other hand, and led him to the door.

"So sorry," she said, looking into the face now blank and limp with reaction. "So sad" — and the man looked at her, and nodded heavily.

"I'll drive him home," Gregory said crisply, and Harriet saw them both into the lift, watching the cage rattle downwards with a sense of despair that she knew would remain with her for a long time, as it always did after those rare occasions when a child died.

As she went back to the kitchen, to check on the teas, and then later, as she went back to the cubicle, alone, to look after the last offices for the dead baby, she thought confusedly about Gregory. This episode had somehow increased his stature in her eyes. He had none of the obvious, almost facile, distress that the medical student had shown, a distress that showed itself in a tendancy to want to run away from such happenings. His pity was real, real enough in spite of his brusque speech and unsmiling face, showing itself in care for the bereaved father, in providing a drink, and making sure the man got home. And that, she told herself, as she looked down at the body of the child when she had finished her job, that was the essence of working in a hospital. You did what you could for each patient, and when you had done that, you turned to care for someone else. And as she later settled the exhausted and over-excited children in their beds for the night, and tidied away the drift of paper wrappings from parcels, the already broken toys, the mess of fallen pine needles from the Christmas tree, she said a confused prayer for the dead child, mixed up with a sort of thanksgiving for being able to find other people to help, even the help she had offered to Anna had been useless.

CHAPTER
SIX

The year drifted gently on its inevitable way, the hospital reflecting the changes of season that happened in the world outside its self-contained life. The pneumonias of the winter months gave way to the increased surgical lists of children who had been waiting for beds to have their operations, and Harriet was busy all day with the rush of admissions, preparations, post-surgical nursing and discharges and the increased activity brought with it.

As spring slowly and reluctantly made way for the warmth of summer, the balcony outside the ward echoed with the shouts of those children well enough to be up and playing about, and the sunshine lit the ward itself into bright patches of light that showed the shabbiness of the old paintwork all too clearly.

But Harriet hardly noticed the passage of time, so thoroughly had she managed to convince herself of the need to live only a day at a time. Her mind refused, now, to think of the future. Each day was sufficient to itself, each day with its work, each evening with Gregory.

And as their relationship ripened, as she came gradually to know him more and more, so she came to respect and lean on his judgement. He still never offered any information about himself, never made any mention of his family if he had one, never talked of any part of his life before he had come to the Royal, and Harriet resolutely never asked him, never questioned his past even remotely. She never even asked him if he had been to a particular restaurant before, if he took her to a new one, meticulously avoiding any line of conversation that might lead logically to reminiscence.

Sometimes, in the deep of the night when she couldn't sleep, when her pillow knotted itself into hard lumps under her restless head, some of her fears would surge upwards, some of her distress about his lack of demonstrativeness would lift its head, and resolutely, she would push it down again. For he still made no attempt to touch her, except in the most impersonal way, handing her into the car, helping her into her coat so that their hands brushed against each other in what was, for Harriet, an electric moment. Yet despite this, she knew that he loved her, knew that he wanted to touch her, to hold her, to kiss her as much as she wanted to respond. She was always aware of the iron control he exercised over himself, the strength of his intention to avoid the physical contact she knew they both needed so much.

Paul, much to her relief, had seemed to accept her loss — if that was how he regarded it — with equanimity. Although he had made no regular attachment with another girl, he was as socially active as ever, appearing at the doctors' mess parties with a different nurse or sister each time, racketing around the hospital in his old insouciant way, greeting Harriet when they met with a casual friendliness that deceived everyone, including Harriet. Only Sally and Stephen knew that his hurt was still there, still very real, though Sally, with unusual taciturnity, said nothing to Harriet about this; she felt, wisely, that it would do no good for Harriet to know of the occasions when Paul burst out bitterly against Gregory to Sally and Stephen, that Harriet had enough to cope with without having to worry about Paul.

Harriet spent a fortnight's holiday in Devonshire, early in April, with her sister and brother-in-law and their delightful children, grateful for the respite in one way, impatient to return to the hospital and Gregory in another.

Sybil, at thirty-three already very matronly, was a little worried at the change in Harriet, perturbed by the way she had seemed to fine down, the way her skin had developed the translucence of thinness, even though the change suited her. Harriet, as Sybil told her husband privately one night, must be in love — really in love. She had become more than just the pretty girl she had always been, had developed a remote beauty that was startling in its delicacy.

But in spite of the closeness of the sisters, a closeness that had developed since the death of their parents many years earlier, Sybil couldn't discover with whom Harriet might be in love, and she had the good sense not to probe.

On the last day of Harriet's holiday, however, as they packed her bags in the middle of the hubbub five children under six can raise when they really try, she did tell Harriet to remember that the Vicarage was her home, and would be as long as she wanted it to be.

"We'll always be here, Hattie," Sybil said, using the childish nickname. "If ever you need us, or you've got any problems, remember that, won't you? And it isn't only me — Edward is as attached to you as I am. So if you need us, or if you've got any — difficulties — give a shout. We'll be listening for it."

Harriet hugged Sybil's plump figure, and clung to her for a moment before thanking her, and promising to remember.

"I don't know myself how things are going to be with me, Sybil, but as soon as I do know, I'll tell you. Bless you for being so understanding. Not one question — and I know you've got lots!" and they laughed together, and Harriet went back to London and the Royal with a warm feeling inside that whatever else happened, Sybil and Edward and their fat babies would always be around to be loved and to love in return.

Gregory met her at the station, his eyes kindling with pleasure at the sight of her head thrust out of the carriage window as the train ground into the huge terminus. And she, in her turn, felt the familiar lurch inside at the first sight of his lean body and grizzled head, a feeling complicated a little by a sudden rush of tenderness. He looked so lonely, standing there against the garish colours of an advertisement hoarding, his rather shabby overcoat hunched round his thin shoulders.

"I've missed you," he said, as he picked up her two cases, and walked beside her to the barrier.

"And I you," she replied, looking up at him, smiling, love in her eyes as naked as a child's. And that was all they did say on a personal level, talking desultorily of hospital doings as they drove back to the hospital, though beneath their casual chatter both were almost painfully aware of the other's physical proximity.

She went on duty next morning with real pleasure, looking forward to the rush of work that was the only thing that really kept her going. It had been the lack of mental preoccupation that had been the hardest thing to bear about her holiday, though she had benefited in a physical way from it, looking more rested than she had for months. Her uniform felt stiff and strange, even after only two weeks out of it, and she stretched her neck against the grip of her starched collar with a sort of masochistic pleasure in the stiffness of it.

Later, at ten o'clock, she was tube feeding a baby in the far isolation cubicle, a two week old scrap of a creature whose hold on life was pathetically precarious. As she manipulated the fine red tube, watched the milk formula drip through the glass connection, all that made her a children's ward sister came bubbling up in her. Nothing she felt, could ever be as rewarding as this, this struggle to care for these children. If they survived — and she was grimly determined that this one certainly would — they would grow up never knowing anything about the woman who had helped to make their lives possible, and for Harriet, this was one of the joys of nursing children. She had always found the gratitude of adult patients she had nursed somehow distasteful. She did her job because she loved it, and to be treated by a patient as though she were a sort of angel of mercy, as many adults did, embarrassed her, took some of the bloom from her pleasure in her job.

As she finished the task, and checked the incubator for temperature and oxygen flow, one of the nurses tapped on the glass partition, and nodded. Harriet came out, leaving the baby to digest its feed and go on with the slow process of healing. She hung her gown outside and as she washed her hands in the basin on the barrier nursing table, the nurse told her of a new admission on his way up.

"It's a bit of an oddity, Sister," the nurse said. "Casualty sister said the police brought him in. He's about five or so, she thinks, but he won't talk — so they don't even know his name. She says the police have no idea who he is — found him wandering around somewhere, and brought him here."

Harriet dried her hands, and sighed a little. "These police really are a bit much," she said crossly. "They treat this hospital as a clearing house for all their problems —"

The nurse grinned. "It's a true bill this time, Sister. I mean, there *is* something wrong with the child," she peered at the scrap of paper in her hand on which she had made a few notes as she had spoken to Casualty sister on the telephone. "He's got some injuries — a few abrasions, a huge bruise on one hip, and query a fracture of a bone in his foot — they're waiting for an X-ray report on that. Sister says she thinks he might have been hurt in a road accident or something —"

"Hmm," Harriet made her way through the ward. "All right, nurse. Put him in bed seven, will you? At five, he's a bit big for a cot, I imagine. I've got to take Casey's stitches out, and then I'll come and see our little mystery. Not that he'll be a mystery for long. They never are. There'll be an agitated parent rushing in any minute, I daresay."

When she brought the little Jamaican boy back from the dressing cubicle, his appendix wound now minus its stitches, and tucked him back into his cot, a piece of chocolate in his hand because he had "been such a good boy and hadn't made a fuss," Harriet turned to bed seven.

At the sight of the child who sat on it, pressed against the white painted iron bars at the head, his knees drawn up, his head down in a classically defensive pose, Harriet's heart twisted with pity. He looked so bereft, so lost, so utterly bewildered in this strange huge room full of oddly dressed people and rows of beds and cots. She picked up a toy from the bottom of Casey's cot, which didn't disturb that small brown child in the least, so plentifully did his adoring parents supply him with toys, and went to sit at the edge of bed seven.

He was small, with fine bones only lightly covered with flesh, and the delicate blueish skin of the very fair. His hair was the colour of spun barley sugar, and lay on his head in a smooth cap that was grimy now with dust and a patch of oil. He had huge blue eyes, the pale china blue that so often goes with very fair hair, and startlingly dark brown lashes, lashes that curled at the edge to a fringe of gold, glinting in the morning sunlight. His face was pointed, the chin held rigid now in an effort to keep his soft mouth firmly closed, and he stared at Harriet with suspicious eyes, trying to shrink into an even smaller ball, pulling back against the bars at the head of the bed as though he would have gone right through them if he could.

"Hello," Harriet said softly.

He sat quite still, never taking his unwinking eyes from her face, making no sign that he had heard her at all.

Gently, Harriet put the little toy engine she was holding in front of him, and for a moment, he looked down at it. Then, seeming to dismiss it as an irrelevance, he raised his eyes to her face again and ignored the engine.

"What's your name, lovey?" Harriet asked softly. Still no response, just that unwinking stare. He might be deaf, Harriet thought. I've seen just this look on the face of a deaf child before now. Surreptitiously, she dropped her hand below the level of the side of the bed, and watching him carefully, snapped her fingers with a sharp crack. The child's eyes shifted briefly towards the sound, then returned to her face. Not deaf then.

She tried another ploy. From her top pocket she pulled a small chocolate bar — for she always carried some, knowing how few children could resist sweet things. She held it out to him, but after a brief glance at it, he ignored it. She took the silver paper off, holding it out again, invitingly, but though he looked longer at the rich brown of the chocolate, he refused to be tempted. So Harriet dropped it onto the bed, and with a smile, stood up. She crossed the ward to stand at the table in the centre, ostensibly busying herself with an injection tray, but watching him covertly from under her lashes. After a while the child stirred a little, looked sharply at her bent and apparently absorbed head, and then picked up the chocolate. For a moment he peered around with the cunning suspicion of a marauding cat, and when he was sure no one was looking at him wolfed the chocolate with a voracious hunger that wrung Harriet's heart with pity. He's starving, poor little devil, she thought. Who on earth could let a child get as hungry as that?

With apparent casualness, she returned to him, sitting again on the edge of the bed, saddened by his immediate shrinking into his corner again.

"Let's play a game, shall we?" she said. "I'll try to guess your name, and if I get it right, you shall have lots and lots of chocolate — piles and piles of it, all you can eat. Shall we?"

Still he made no response, but Harriet persisted.

"Andrew? Adam? Barry? Billy? Charles? Craig? —" Working through the alphabet, she said name after name, trying desperately to remember the sort of names that had been fashionable to give little boys about five years ago, the sort of name he might be expected to have. But it was useless. He showed no sign of recognition at any name, not for a moment giving that faint flicker that Harriet was watching for so closely, that slight movement of muscle that she knew would show his recognition of familiar syllables.

From behind her, a voice said, "Hello, Sister. Trying to solve our little mystery, are you?"

She got to her feet. "Good morning, Dr Bennett," she said formally, and the senior paediatrician smiled down at her from his considerable height, and said, "Glad to see you back. Had a good holiday?"

"Very pleasant, thank you sir," she said, and they moved away to the centre of the ward, where Dr Bennett perched himself against the table, and swung a long leg idly as he looked across at the child in bed seven. "Casualty told me about this child. Very odd altogether."

"The police brought him in?"

"Mmm. But not before they had tried very hard to find his people. I don't know the details — apparently there's a policewoman on her way up from Casualty to see me about him. I told them I'd be here in a few minutes, so they said —"

The double doors swung, and a fair girl in the neat blue uniform of a woman police constable came down the ward, her heavy shoes clacking noisily on the wooden floor.

Dr Bennett stood up, and nodded at her, and the policewoman smiled back, pulling her notebook from her pocket.

"They told me you were the best person to talk to about this child, sir," she said. "We picked him up at six o'clock last night, down at the market —"

"The market?" Dr Bennett interrupted.

"Street market, sir, at the corner of High Road and Jefferson Street."

"Not far from the underground station," Harriet said. "I know it. Mostly fruit and vegetables, and a couple of gimcrack stalls and old clothes stalls —"

"That's it, Sister. Well, we got a call. This child had taken some fruit from one of the stalls, and the stall-holder had caught him. And when he couldn't get any sense out of him, he called us — it's as well he did.

Well, we couldn't find out who he was, and the station sergeant said seeing no one had reported a missing child, and he looked a bit small just to be wandering on his own, we'd better put out a search for his people. We tried all evening, put him in a bed at the station, and waited for someone to claim him. Well, sir, no one did — and that's really odd. We've never had a child of this age so long without *someone* reporting him missing."

"Quite." Dr Bennett frowned. "Six o'clock last night, you say? Hasn't he said anything at all since then?"

"Not a word, sir. Wouldn't eat, either, though we tried all we could to make him — anyway, he slept all right, and this morning we put out an all stations call to check on missing kids. He's not been reported anywhere, it seems, and we've covered the area very carefully. They're checking outside London now. Well, sir, this morning, I thought the kid ought to —" she blushed suddenly. "Well, sir, he hadn't been to the lavatory since we got him to the station, sir, and we haven't any kids' clothes if there's any accident, so I took him. He fought like a mad thing —" and she held out a scratched hand ruefully. "But I managed to get his pants off, sir, and sit him on the lav — the toilet. And then I saw the bruise. So we thought we'd better bring him here."

"Hmm," Dr Bennett nodded. "As well you did, constable. He's got several abrasions, and a badly bruised foot. They had some trouble trying to X-ray him, I gather, so I don't suppose the films'll show much — but it seems possible he's fractured a metatarsal. We'll get the orthopods to have a look at that. In the meantime, we'll keep him in, and try our best to get him to talk to us. If you hear from his people, you'll notify us, of course —"

The policewoman, clearly relieved at being rid of her burden, took herself off, and Harriet and Dr Bennett returned to the child's bedside.

He had made no move at all, still sitting crouched against the head of the bed, his eyes staring around him with a lack lustre look that was pathetic in its emptiness. Dr Bennett tried to persuade the child to talk, but after ten minutes of gentle urging, he sighed and stood up.

"Completely withdrawn, Sister," he said. "No contact at all, is there? Look, treat those abrasions in the usual way, watch him for any signs of other disease — it's possible he was in an accident and those abrasions certainly look as though they were the result of a bad tumble which might have inflicted some internal injury, and I'll get the orthopods to see his foot. He's all yours, Sister. Perhaps when he's been here a while you'll be able to make some contact with him. Offer him some loving — you know the sort of thing I mean — and try to get him to talk. And see the night staff observe him carefully. Children who refuse to talk while they're awake sometimes talk in their sleep. Right?"

Harriet nodded, then suddenly she said, "We'll have to call him something, sir. We can't just say 'you' all the time, can we? Not very loving —"

Dr Bennett looked down at the silent child, and sighed sharply. "Yes —" then he smiled a little grimly. "He's come to us out of the blue, Sister — a gift from the gods, if you like. Call him Theodore, hmm? The gift of God."

Harriet smiled too. "A shade — stiff, sir?" she ventured. "Could we shorten that perhaps? Tod, say?"

Dr Bennett laughed, and nodded. "You are quite right, my dear. Tod it is. Nice and simple. It'll do till we find out what it really should be. I hope it won't be long before we do —"

And after he had gone, Harriet stood at the door, looking down the ward at the slight little boy in bed seven, and silently agreed with him. No one should be as unhappy, as lost, as abandoned, as this pale fair scrap of a child. Tod, she thought. An anonymous sounding syllable for an anonymous child. I hope someone claims him, soon.

CHAPTER
SEVEN

But no one did. The police checked with every station in the country, but Tod fitted none of the descriptions of such children as were missing. The aid of newspapers and television was sought and Tod's thin little face stared out from front pages, from television screens, and still no one came to say they knew him, let alone claim him.

A special court was convened in the hospital, and Tod was solemnly described as an infant in need of care and protection, and put under the impersonal guardianship of the State.

"It's all we can do, Sister." Dr Bennett told Harriet, afterwards. "This way, we can at least treat him properly — if he needs surgery for example — which he doesn't as it happens — we'll be able to perform an operation with the Court's consent. But it's an odd business. I'd have thought someone somewhere would have recognised his photograph —"

"What will happen to him?" Harriet asked practically.

Dr Bennett shrugged. "We'll get him physically fit, first, of course. Then I suppose we'll have to get the trick-cyclist on to his mental condition." Dr Bennett had all the old fashioned physician's fine scorn of psychiatrists. "This refusal to speak could be the result of a traumatic experience — the accident, whatever it was, that gave him those injuries — or it could be a form of juvenile amnesia. I'm not much up on this sort of thing, quite honestly."

"Then we'll keep him here?" Harriet persisted.

"Not for long, Sister. I suppose they'll find a vacancy in some institution for him — one for the mentally handicapped perhaps —"

"Oh, no!" Harriet said. "Surely not! He mayn't talk, but he's not lacking in intelligence — I'm sure of that."

Dr Bennett looked at her shrewdly. "Don't get too attached to him, my dear," he said gently. "He's a pathetic little creature, I know, but we can't keep him here indefinitely. This is an acute hospital, you know — not a depository for unwanted children."

Harriet, forced to agree, watched Dr Bennett go, and went back to Tod's bed, to sit beside him and look with a frustrated sympathy at his silent face. They had made some progress with him, and little as it was, Harriet felt a little cheered as she thought about it.

With infinite patience on her part, she had managed to coax him to eat, putting all the most tempting things she could think of in front of him. Once he had tried something — and Harriet had given him a paper packet of potato crisps, knowing how most children adored them — and had reassured himself that the food she gave him was really meant for him, that he wouldn't be punished for eating it, he ate hungrily, refusing nothing, drinking hugely, filling his small frame as full as he could.

But that was all. He refused to play, ignoring every toy they gave him, looking at the brightly coloured books or playthings on his bed as though they were objects he had never seen in his life before. All day, he would sit in the corner of his bed, his legs drawn up, just sitting, making no response to any overtures, even from the other children. Some of them would come and stand by his bed, talking to him, but his refusal to respond chilled them, and they would drift away, back to their toys and other friends, shunning the silent boy in bed seven.

Harriet had tried to get him to walk, but when she lifted him out of bed, putting a dressing gown onto him, fitting slippers onto his little feet, he just stood there, making no effort either to return to bed, or move away from it. He had let the orthopaedic surgeon examine his feet (and fortunately, there was no fracture to be found) had allowed Harriet to put a supportive bandage on the swelling without fighting, but that had been all.

There was one good sign, Harriet thought, leaning forward to move a toy near to him, in the forlorn hope that this time he would respond. He had some control over his body, still had some social ability. She had put a potty beside his bed, and gone away, watching him from out of his line of vision, and been glad to see him use it. Whatever had happened to him, it hadn't had the all too common effect of making him incontinent.

She leaned forward suddenly, and with an impulsive but gentle grasp, lifted the child out of his corner, and held him on her lap. He did not resist her, but sat there, his legs held stiffly in front of him, his back rigid, staring ahead of him in silence.

Slowly, Harriet began to rock to and fro, her arms about the slender little body, and under her breath at first, then more audibly, she began to croon a song at him. Quite why she chose the song she did, she never knew, but she found herself singing an old popular song called the *Umbrella Man*. "Any umbrellas, any umbrellas to mend today — he'll mend your umbrellas and go on his way singing — any umbrellas, any umbrellas —"

The child on her lap shuddered slightly, then, to Harriet's intense joy, his body began to relax. She made no sign that she had noticed, just crooned on, rocking at the same rhythm.

And gradually, Tod softened, gradually his head dropped towards her till his fair smooth hair was just beneath her chin, nestling against the starch of her apron. His legs came up under him, and he thrust the two middle fingers of one hand into his mouth, until he was curled on her lap, sucking at his hand like a child of half his apparent age.

And soon he slept, but Harriet crooned on until she was sure he was fast asleep. When her staff nurse came over at a sign from Harriet, she looked a little surprised.

"Look Staff!" Harriet whispered. "This is the first time this child has shown any appreciation of any human contact. And I don't want to spoil it. I'll have to sit here till he wakes up. Maybe he'll talk to me then. Can you manage to finish off and get the children settled? There's the tube feed for the baby in the end cubicle and the skin prep for tomorrow's orthopaedic list —" rapidly she gave her instructions, and sent the nurses scurrying round the ward on the evening's tasks, and still Tod sat on her lap, his head under her chin, and slept on.

She called one of the nurses to tuck a blanket over Tod's small body, and watched the nurses settle the children into bed, watched the light diminish as each window blind was pulled down, saw the familiar evening face of the ward appear as the red shaded central lights were put on, and the children were tucked in for the long night's sleep ahead of them.

She listened to them all, carefully flexing her stiff legs and arms, doing her best not to wake the sleeping child on her lap, listened to the odd snufflings and little moans that sleeping children always seem to produce, and smiled a little as she listened. It was almost like a room full of small snuffling furry animals, she thought. Warm, baby ones.

And then, just a little while before the night nurses were due to come on duty, Gregory's white-coated shape came through the big double doors. He looked round with the characteristic swift appraising look she knew so well, and came over to her as soon as he could make out where she was in the dim light.

He leaned on the foot of the bed, smiling a little at the sight of her, sitting there in a low bedside chair, a blanketed child on her lap.

"It suits you," he said in a low voice. "You both look — right, somehow. Did you know it suited you to have a child on your lap? Is that why you work with sick kids?" and his dark eyes glinted at her with rare humour.

She gave a soft snort of laughter. "Of course. And I always choose blonde children to sit with," she said. "They suit me best of all."

"Couldn't you just put him to bed now? He's flat out. And we're supposed to be going out to dinner tonight. Had you forgotten?"

Harriet smiled up at him. "I haven't forgotten. But I'm hoping he'll wake up before long, and maybe talk to me."

"Talk to you?" he sounded puzzled.

"Haven't you heard about our small mystery?" Harriet asked. "This is the child the police brought us—"

He came round the bed to perch on the edge and peer into the sleeping child's face.

"I did hear something — what's it all about? I haven't had many patients on this ward this week, so I haven't been around much —"

Briefly, she told him, about how Tod was found; the way no one had come to claim him, and Gregory's face softened as he listened. "Poor little monkey," he murmured. "I can't imagine how people can be so cruel. Someone somewhere must belong to him. To abandon him so —"

Harriet looked down at the child, and nodded. "I know," she said softly. "I couldn't do it, no matter what happened — I couldn't do it —"

"He's fast asleep, Harriet," Gregory said, after a long pause. "Are you going to sit with him all night? Because I shouldn't think he'd wake before morning now —"

"I suppose not —" she stirred experimentally, and very carefully stood up, still holding Tod gently, but he didn't wake. Gregory pulled the blankets back, and she put the child into bed, tucking him into the covers with a careful touch. Tod moved a little, snuffled softly, and slept on.

They stood together for a moment, looking down on the fair head, the golden edged fringe of long lashes that shaded the thin cheeks, and then Harriet stretched a little.

"I did so hope he would wake," she said regretfully. "I thought perhaps that I could talk to him while he was still half asleep, and get him to say something. Anything. I'm sure if I can once get him started on speech, we'll be able to find out about him — he just needs to start —"

Gregory looked at her in the half light, and said softly, "You're getting very fond of him?"

"He's so alone," Harriet said defensively. "So lost. I can't bear the thought of him going to an institution somewhere. Oh, I know they're good places, that they do their best, but —"

"I know," Gregory looked down at Tod's sleeping face. "I can understand how you must feel about him. But it isn't much use, is it? You can't adopt him —"

All through their dinner that evening, Harriet was abstracted, somehow unable to keep her thoughts away from the child sleeping in bed seven, for once less concerned with Gregory than with her job. Gregory, with the swift understanding she was coming to value in him, didn't seem to mind her abstraction, only saying, as he said goodnight, "I hope your Tod is claimed soon, Harriet. As much for your sake as his. It's not much fun being as miserable about a patient as you are about him."

And Harriet had smiled up at him gratefully, and on an impulse put her hand up to touch his face; more from gratitude for his understanding than because of her ever-present need to touch him, to have some physical

79

contact with him. But he had made a tiny movement, an almost instinctive rearing back, and a little chilled, she had dropped her hand, and said "Thank you, Gregory. Good night," and gone to bed, unhappy and bewildered again, the ache in her heart sharpened by his lack of response.

If she had thought about it at all, she had certainly never thought that anything Gregory could do or say could make her any more bewildered and unhappy about him than she was. Until the next morning.

A child with a suspected intussusception was sent up from Casualty as an emergency at half past nine, and as Gregory was the surgical registrar on call, Harriet sent a message to the mess for him.

He came promptly, and with all the gentle skill that Harriet found one of the most wonderful things about him, examined the child, and managed to soothe the frightened parents with a few words, arranging to operate later that afternoon. It was when they had finished with the child, while Harriet and Gregory were walking down the ward towards the office, that it happened.

The ward was unusually quiet for once, many of the children being out on the sunny balcony, listening to the hospital school teacher read a story to them. The few children still in bed in the ward were sleeping, or just lying quietly staring at the ceiling thinking the imponderable thoughts of the very young.

Then, above the crisp fall of their footsteps, a voice said "Greg — Greg."

Puzzled, Harriet turned, and looked back down the ward.

Tod was sitting bolt upright, his thin face unusually flushed, his chin up, staring at Gregory with an intensity that made his blue eyes seem to blaze. And then, never taking his eyes from Gregory, who had himself turned to stare at the child, Tod moved forwards, sliding his thin legs over the side of the bed, to stand swaying a little beside it.

He looked oddly adult somehow, despite the way his gaily coloured pyjamas hung on his thin frame, the way the trouser legs creased themselves over his narrow feet. He stood still for a moment, and then started to walk, a little wobbly on his legs, legs that had not moved of their own volition in all the three days he had been in the ward, and came pattering barefooted over the polished wooden floor towards them.

For Harriet, time seemed to stand still. In the quiet sunny stillness she watched Tod come towards them, watched his hair blaze and fade alternately as he went past each bright window, watched his eyes, their intensely blue gaze never faltering from the face of the man who stood as still as herself beside her.

Tod came to stand in front of Gregory, staring up at him and put a hand out tentatively.

"Greg?" he said again, his voice high and thin, the voice of a frightened bird. "Greg?"

Gregory looked down at the child, his face closed and expressionless. Then he moved, stepped back, and said in a voice that sounded strangely thick to Harriet, "What? What did you say?"

Tod's hand dropped and he stood quite still, watchful and suddenly on guard again.

"Greg," he said again. "Greg. Greg. Greg."

Harriet, her head feeling empty and suddenly light, managed to move, to drop on her knees beside Tod, to put an arm round his narrow shoulders, managed to turn her head so that she could look up at Gregory, suddenly seeming to tower above her like a giant.

"What is it — who — you know him, Gregory?" her voice came huskily, forcing its way past the constriction in her throat.

Gregory never took his eyes from the child's face. For a long moment there was silence, then he said roughly. "Know him? Of course I don't. I never saw him before in my life."

In the circle of her arm the child never moved, even though she tightened her grasp on him, ignoring her as if she were no more than a fly that had alighted on his shoulder.

"But —" Harriet felt as though she were lost, groping in a huge dark room, a room with neither walls nor ceiling, just an infinity of blackness. "But he said your name — he knows you."

Gregory thrust his hands deep into the pockets of his white coat, and with a voice devoid of any expression said again, "I never saw him before in my life. Never."

"Greg," Tod said again, in the same flat monotone, no question in his voice now. "Greg. Greg. Greg."

"I tell you he knows *you*," Harriet cried, her voice high and shrill. "It's the first time he's spoken — and all

82

he says is your name! He knows you, Gregory — *he knows you!*"

Gregory looked at her now, his eyes deeply shadowed, so that she could read nothing in their sombre depths.

"I tell you I never saw him before in my life. I'll tell theatre about that intussusception, Sister. Have him ready for two o'clock, will you?" and without looking at Tod again, he turned, and walked from the ward, his footsteps loud in the silence.

Together, Tod and Harriet watched him go, both of them seeming frozen into immobility, both staying quite still long after the double doors had stopped their slow diminishing swing behind Gregory's figure, long after they heard the lift gates clatter open and closed, heard the lift whine away to the ground floor of the hospital.

CHAPTER
EIGHT

In a way, Harriet was grateful for the afternoon's rush of work. In addition to the child who was to go to theatre at two o'clock, three children were admitted from Casualty just after lunch suffering from coal gas poisoning. A fractured gas main near their home had sent them, together with their mother, into the Royal in a state of collapse that was ominous.

Paul, as the medical registrar on emergency call for the week, came to the ward with them, together with his junior houseman, and the three children, the oldest of whom was just five, the youngest under a year, kept them and Harriet extended at full pitch until long after seven o'clock.

By then, when Harriet could at last relax a little, she was too exhausted to think very much about Gregory and Tod — indeed, the long struggle to keep the youngest child, who had suffered most from the gas fumes, just breathing, had wrung her dry of any feeling.

She followed Paul from the big cubicle where the three children were being nursed together, trailing wearily behind him through the darkened ward, past each shadowed bed, past Tod's humped shape in bed seven, her head spinning with fatigue, the faint sickly smell of gas still seeming to linger in her nostrils.

Paul subsided into the armchair in her office, while she sat down at her desk and began to write the ward report ready for the night staff. He watched her in silence, only stirring to grab gratefully at the coffee a sympathetic junior nurse brought to them both, watching Harriet above the rim of his cup as she sat with bent head, scribbling away at her report.

"I think they'll do," he said at length, when she had finished, dropping her pen to flex cramped fingers. "That baby had me more than a little worried for a while. It must have been a hell of a leak —"

"It was," Harriet told him. "The ambulance man who brought them in told Casualty Sister that their house was next to that new development up by the rope factory — you know where I mean? He said it couldn't have been more than half an hour the house was full of gas — seems they knew what had happened on the building site — they'd used a charge of explosive to shift a main wall they were demolishing, and it cracked a main supply pipe. And for these kids to get enough to have this effect on them, it must have been a hell of a big pipe —"

Paul reached for the 'phone. "Phillips was looking after the mother. I'd better see how she is —"

The report from Women's Medical was fortunately a good one; the mother had been deeply unconscious for some hours, but now she too was out of the wood, and beginning to regain consciousness, and Harriet smiled a little tremulously at Paul when he hung up the 'phone, and passed the information on to her.

"Thank God for that," she said wearily. "It would have been too awful if the three of them had lost their mother —"

"Mmm," Paul yawned widely, cracking his jaws and stretching luxuriously. "Bad enough to have one apparent orphan in the ward, without three more — how *are* things with your mystery child? Have they found his people yet?"

All Harriet's misery came flooding back at his question. She sat still, her head bent, looking down at her desk, trying to get her thoughts into some sort of order. She knew what she ought to do; Tod had spoken for the first time, and she should tell Dr Bennett about it, so that the police could be told, so that Gregory could be officially questioned about him. She had the first clue to the child's identity, and she ought to see that this important clue was properly followed up. But Gregory — unconsciously, she straightened, and raised her head to look directly at Paul.

"No," she said evenly. "He's still a mystery. They haven't found his people yet."

"It's a problem," Paul said. "What'll happen to him? Will they send him to a home somewhere?"

"I don't know," Harriet said. "He's still not ready to be discharged from the ward — those abrasions aren't quite healed yet. I — suppose Dr Bennett will decide what to do when he *is* ready."

He got to his feet, and stood for a moment looking down at her. "Harriet —" he began. "Harriet —"

She looked up at him, at the familiar face she had once found so exciting, and thought vaguely, he's a nice man. I wish — I wish I could have cared for him —

86

"How are things, Harriet?" Paul said awkwardly. "I'm not prying — really I'm not. But I'm fond of you, you know. A friend. I just wondered — you're looking a bit peaky."

"Just fatigued," Harriet smiled at him a little shyly. "Just a bit tired, that's all. Occupational hazard with nurses, isn't it? But I'm fine —"

"I suppose it is," he said soberly. "Though it isn't like you to look quite so — bothered. Look, Harriet —" He stopped, and then said with shyness that sat oddly on his handsome face, "Don't forget that I *am* your friend, will you? I'm interested in you, and if I can ever be of any help — well, just ask."

She managed a bright smile that stretched her stiff lips a little painfully. "Help? What sort of help would I need, Paul? I'm fine — really I am —"

"Oh, I don't know. You look so — hag-ridden. As though you've got to carry the world and his wife on your back. It doesn't suit you. So if you ever need a shoulder to cry on, I've got a pair of the most absorbent shoulders in the business —"

"Thank you, Paul," she said softly. "I'll remember," and with a curt nod, he turned and went, disappearing through the double doors with a flick of his white coat.

For a moment, she wanted to run after him, to accept his offer, to rest her tired head on his broad shoulder and tell him of her misery, of what had happened that morning with Tod and Gregory, to throw all her worries on to him, to relax in the sure comfort of his affection for her.

And then she shook herself a little impatiently. It's no good, she told herself. Gregory is my problem, and no one else can help me but Gregory himself.

For a while, she sat with her chin propped on her fists staring unseeingly at her reflection in the glass wall of her office, trying to decide what to do. But her thoughts went round in circles, persistently coming back to the same point. I'll have to talk to Gregory about it — ask him — *make* him tell me how Tod knew his name, force him to explain. I can put up with just so much secretiveness and no more. He'll have to explain.

She pulled her eyes down, to look at the 'phone beside her elbow, sitting black and mute waiting for her to pick it up. With a conscious physical effort she reached out her hand, and started to dial the mess number, then stopped. I don't want to have to ask someone to get him for me, she thought. If I have to sit here and hold on while they get him, I'll hang up — I won't have the courage to wait. Instead, she dialled the switchboard, and asked the impersonal voice at the other end to put Gregory's call lights on, and then hung up, to sit staring at the panel above the ward door as it started to flick a red light on and off, the red light that would tell Gregory to contact switchboard.

After a long moment, the light stopped, and then the 'phone rang, shrilly, beside her. She looked at it, and with her heart beating with a sick thumping that made her want to run away, she picked up the receiver.

"You wanted me?" Even with the distortion of the 'phone, his voice carried deep tones that made her shiver with pleasure.

"Yes — yes," she managed. "Gregory — I want to see you."

"Is something wrong with that intussusception child?" His voice was distant, a little unfriendly.

"No. He's fine. Round from his anaesthetic and sleeping quietly. This — this is something else. I must see you."

There was a long silence, so long that she said, "Gregory?" a little uncertainly.

"I'll meet you by the gate to the Nurses' Home garden. In ten minutes. Will that do?" he said.

"Half an hour would be better," she said. "I'll have to give the report to the night staff —"

"Very well," he said shortly, and hung up, leaving her listening stupidly to the high buzz of the dialling tone.

She waited for the night staff, giving them the report, telling them what to do about the post-operative child and the gassed children with her usual efficiency, while a heavy lump of fear pressed thickly in her chest. The coldness of Gregory's voice, the chill that had come through the 'phone at her, made her feel icy herself. He will tell me to mind my own business, she thought miserably, tell me that I have no right to question him. And that will be the end of everything. All he wants from me is patience, an unquestioning patience, and now I'm nagging him, and he won't ever want to take me out again, and the future will be empty. That will be the end.

And then her basic common sense asserted itself, made her feel strong again. I have every right to question him, she told herself firmly. Whatever the explanation is, I have a right to ask for it. Quite apart from our relationship, there's Tod to consider. And right now, he matters more than my feelings.

So it was with a strong step that she made her way towards the Nurses' Home, her cape pulled closely round her against the cold night air. No high emotion, she promised herself. No accusations. I'll just ask him, calmly, to explain.

He was leaning against the gate as she got there, his face lit with the glow of a cigarette. He dropped it as she arrived, to grind it out under his foot, and after a momentary pause, followed her through the gate.

The garden was empty, the faint rattle of dry branches in the trees making the only movement there was. Harriet led the way to one of the wooden benches that a grateful patient had donated to the hospital, and sat down in a corner, to huddle herself even deeper into her cape. He sat down at the other end of it and she could feel his eyes on her in the darkness.

"We won't be interrupted here," she said, her voice high and thin. "And I must talk to you."

"Well." There was no question in his voice, no apparent awareness of her tension, her anxiety.

She bit her lip, putting out her hand towards him for a moment. Then, when he made no attempt to move, no sign that he had seen her gesture, she dropped it, and said evenly, "It's about Tod."

"Well," he said again.

"Gregory, not so very long ago, you told me — asked me to be patient with you. You — you gave me some reason to believe that you felt a little about me as I do about you, but you made it clear that I would have to wait for some time before — before you could talk to me, either about your own feelings, or mine. And I accepted that." She stopped, and looked across at him, at the faint glimmer of his white coat in the darkness, the dull gleam of the stethoscope that was sticking out of his pocket. He made no move, sitting there still and silent, his eyes still on her.

Painfully, she began to speak again. "Well, that was all right. I — I care enough for you to wait. But now — now it would seem that other factors are involved. When it was just a matter of you and me — just my own unhappiness, I could cope, could manage not to question you. No one suffered but me. Now — it's different." She leaned forwards, trying to see some flicker of response in his dark face. "Don't you see, Gregory? This child *knows you*. He's a lost child — no one seems to care about what happens to him. And if he knows you, it's obvious you know him. And however much you may deny it, it's pretty obvious to *me* that this — acquaintanceship between you has some bearing on the situation as it stands between us."

Still he made no answer, no movement.

"Gregory — help me!" she let her unhappiness show in her voice, despite her promise to herself that there would be no high emotion in this conversation. "Give me credit for some understanding, Gregory! Don't shut yourself away from me! Tell me what it is — tell me who this child *is*, what he is to you, *who* he is! I'm not just asking you for my own satisfaction, Gregory, believe me I'm not. If you don't want to tell me about whatever it is that makes you so secretive, I don't want to know. But this child — he matters, Gregory! I've got to know who he is, where his mother is, find out why he's been abandoned. He's not just a — a cipher. He's a person — and a bitterly lost person at that. In all decency, Gregory, you've got to tell me!"

In the silence that followed, she seemed to be able to hear every tiny movement in the dark garden, the faint chatter of dry branches, the soft whisper as the wind moved the leaves of the flowers in the dark beds lining the lawn, and beyond, the ever present muted thunder of traffic on the main road that flanked the hospital. Then, he moved.

"I told you this morning that I had never seen this child in my life before, Harriet. You don't believe that." It was a statement, not a question.

"How can I?" she asked miserably. "How can I? It can't be mere coincidence. If yours was a common name, perhaps — perhaps it could be. But Gregory isn't a common name — and he said 'Greg' as clearly as it could be said. And his recognition of you was the first sign of any — any real response he had made. That, and your name — obviously he knew you! You must see that. And how could he know you if you never saw him before?"

"I don't know," his voice was still flat, still cold. "I'm as mystified as you are."

"Oh for Christ's sake!" she was angry now, bitterly angry. "Do you take me for a complete idiot, man? Do you think I'm the sort of besotted creature that will accept *everything* without question? I may have made myself look a fool, may have grovelled in front of you

— but I haven't lost every vestige of intelligence just because I'm stupid enough to love you —"

He moved then, leaned towards her, "Don't, Harriet, don't — please."

But she was too angry now to heed the sudden note of pain in his voice. "You — you, a doctor! You're supposed to care for people, you're supposed to be giving your life to caring for the sick. And all you care about is your own self-centred need! Never mind what happens to other people — as long as Gregory Weston can live his life safely wrapped up away from other people, the rest can go to hell! What you're doing to *me* is bad enough — but I'm damned if I'll let you get away with treating this child as you are. And I'm warning you, Gregory. Either you tell me right now who this child is, or I find out myself — somehow. I'll find out — and I don't care if you do get hurt in the process —"

Suddenly he was close beside her, his hands on her shoulders, gripping her through the thick fabric of her cape so hard that she winced.

"Listen to me — listen to me, Harriet! You must believe me! *I don't know who this child is.* He's a complete stranger to me. Selfish I may be — but even I couldn't lie about this. I have — I haven't ever seen him before —"

She looked up at him, at his face so close to her own, closer than it had ever been.

"But — but you must have some idea —" she said a little uncertain now, convinced almost against her will by the urgency of his tone, the note of truth that burned in his words.

He dropped his hands then, and said, "Perhaps — but the idea I have won't help. I — even if I knew his mother once, it's been a long time. I had thought — oh, what's the use." He turned his head away from her, to stare up at the trees. "It's over now. Finished. Whatever happens now, it's finished. I can't see you again, Harriet. I'll have to leave here, now. I couldn't bear to go on seeing you about the hospital, and not be able to — ever see you outside it. And I can't — not now."

Her heart twisted sharply at the sense of loss he transmitted in his voice, and without thinking, she put her arms round him, pulling him close to her, so that his head came down to rest on her shoulder.

For a moment he resisted, and then, almost as though against his will, his own arms went round her, and his cold lips were on hers, kissing her with a hunger, a need, that seemed to cry aloud in the silence.

For a long moment, they clung together, locked in an embrace that carried Harriet away, made her whole body seem to melt in a rush of sensations she had never felt before.

He raised his head then, to pull her roughly against him, to murmur brokenly into her ear words she couldn't hear, words that didn't matter. All she knew was that she loved him, that she needed him.

And then, with a suddenness that left her gasping, he stood up.

"It's no good, Harriet," his voice was harsh again. "No good. It won't work —"

She stared up at him, and said softly. "But it will. It must. I love you, Gregory. And you love me. You can't escape that —"

"Yes — I love you," he said hopelessly. "But I'll have to get over that — somehow. I'm sorry, Harriet."

She shook her head. "No," she said. "No. Whatever it is that makes you so — so unhappy, you'll have to tell me. And you might as well tell me now. Nothing is as bad as it seems if it's put into words —"

But she was talking to empty air. He had turned and gone, his lean body melting into the shadows of the garden, leaving her alone on the wooden bench, her mouth still feeling his kiss, still hurting from the roughness of the urgent passion she had felt in him.

For a long time, she sat there. And all she could think was "Tod. He still hasn't told me. What do I do about Tod?"

CHAPTER
NINE

She spent a miserable sleepless night, tossing and turning through the long hours, grateful when the Sisters' maid arrived with her early tea, one of the few extra privileges the Sisters at the Royal enjoyed. She was still undecided, still not sure what she should do about Tod, as she pinned her apron round her, fixed her cap on her head with unsteady fingers. As she dusted powder on her face, trying to cover the blue shadows under her eyes, the little porcelain girl on the dressing table looked out into the room, her delicate face seeming to hold an aloofness that suddenly made Harriet angry. With a childishness she recognised in herself, a childishness that somehow made her even angrier, she thrust the pretty thing and its laughing-eyed companion into the top drawer, hiding them under her handkerchiefs. Gregory's gifts seemed to mock her now, and she couldn't bear even to look at them.

On an impulse, she decided to call in at the theatres as she went on duty. With luck, Sally would have a few moments to talk to her, and Harriet felt a very definite need of some of Sally's calm good sense.

The theatres were humming with activity as she came through the swinging double doors, nurses already in the tight caps and light cotton dresses and white socks and plimsolls they would wear through the day's operations. As Harriet took in the atmosphere of the place, the gleaming green tiles, the huge instrument cupboards glowing with the cold chrome of equipment, the bubbling of the sterilisers in the annexe, she wished for a moment that she, like Sally, had decided to work in the theatres. No patients to get involved with, she thought bleakly. Just things — and no one can get unhappy about things. People are more complicated.

Sally was checking a tray of instruments, chivvying a rather scared junior as she counted them.

"You'll need twelve haemostats of this size, Nurse. Do you suppose Mr Best will wait about for you to boil up more in the middle of the operation? And for heaven's sake, girl, what size clamp do you call this? We're removing an appendix, not a horse's guts —" The junior flushed miserably under her mask, and scuttled off to correct her errors, as Sally caught sight of Harriet standing at the door, and came over to her.

"I don't know where Matron finds these girls, really I don't," she grumbled. "Nurses today haven't the wit they were born with. When we were in training —"

"Bully," Harriet said, smiling at Sally's cross face in spite of herself. "You were just as dumb as they are now — and you know it."

Sally grinned back. "I suppose so. Now, ducky. To what do I owe the honour of your presence? If you want to borrow the sucker again, we're using it till ten —"

"No —" Harriet followed her into the anaesthetic room, and watched Sally as she began to check the machines, sending gas hissing through the connections as she expertly turned each cylinder on and off. "I need a bit of advice."

"Ask away —" Sally said, and stumbling a little over her words, Harriet told her of what had happened, of Gregory's flat denial that he knew anything about Tod, despite Tod's obvious recognition of him. Told her everything except of Gregory's kiss the night before, his statement that he would have to leave the Royal. That episode was too personal, and its implications too confused even to think about, let alone talk about, even to Sally.

Sally listened in silence, and when Harriet's voice died away, she looked up at her friend shrewdly and smiled at her. "You don't really want my advice, Harriet. What you want is for me to listen while you tell me what you're going to do about this business. So tell me. I'm listening."

Unwillingly, Harriet said, "I don't want to start anything I can't control, Sal. I mean — suppose I do tell Dr Bennett what Tod said — and he puts the police on to Gregory? However I felt about him — if he was no more to me than just a member of the staff, I'd hate to do that when he so obviously doesn't want me to."

"It would be a bit — sneaky," Sally admitted. "But aren't you being a bit schoolgirlish about this? What matters most? Tod, or an old fashioned notion of honour that if you follow it will leave Tod just where he is — unknown and unwanted? That's the real crux."

Harriet nodded unhappily, and began to walk towards the door. "I'd better get on duty," she said. "I suppose you're right, Sal. I just wish there was another way to find out — on my own, without going running to Dr Bennett and through him to the police.,

Behind her, Sally said with a diffidence that Harriet could almost feel. "I — I suppose you've realised what this could mean, Harriet? You know so little about Gregory, don't you? He — Tod could be — related to him," she finished awkwardly.

Without turning, Harriet said evenly, "You mean Tod could be his child? Yes, I've thought about that. It's that that makes it — worse, somehow."

"I imagine it would," Sally said dryly. "If I were you, I'd want to cut your precious Gregory's throat for him. But as I've said before, you and me — we just don't function in the same way."

And as she made her way up to her own ward, Harriet thought bleakly, I wish I were as uncomplicated as Sally. But I'm not. And the possibility that Tod is Gregory's child makes me care even more about what happens. I love Gregory enough to love his child — even another woman's child — But she pushed the thought away, sickened suddenly by the vision that came unsought to her mind, a vision of a happy, Gregory, loving another woman, loving her more than Harriet, loving her enough to —

The ward was buzzing with activity as she came through the door, children bumbling about in their usual way, nurses feeding toddlers with plates of porridge and scrambled eggs, the ward maid lackadaisically pushing cots about as she started the day's cleaning. Harriet took the report from the tired night nurses, before sending them off to their breakfast and well earned sleep, and started her morning's round of her patients. The gassed children were lively this morning, showing little evidence of the state they had been in the night before, and the oldest asked her eagerly if she could see her Mummy. Harriet 'phoned the women's medical ward, and asked if the children could see their mother, and was told that the woman was much better this morning, and would be better still for the sight of her family. So the three children were wrapped in blankets, piled into one big wheelchair, and sent with a nurse to see their mother, bouncing joyously as they went, in imminent danger of tipping the chair and themselves down into a pile of kicking arms and legs.

Harriet smiled as she saw them on their way, relieved for them that they had survived their experience so well, and turned back to the ward to see the rest of the children. The child who had had his operation the day before was doing well, though feeling a little weepy and irritable, and Harriet promised him that his parents would be coming to see him very soon. As she tucked the miserable little creature more comfortably into his blankets, she could see Tod across the ward, sitting as usual in the corner of his bed, watching the children in the ward with his usual disinterested stare. Almost furtively, almost against her will, she watched him, trying to see some resemblance to Gregory in him. Was that how Gregory held his head? How his eyes were set in his face? But even with her now firm belief that this child was Gregory's son, she could see nothing of him in the small fair head, the wide blue eyes, and narrow face with its pointed chin.

There was a squeal from some of the older children as old Nickie, the hospital's elderly postman, came padding into the ward, his hands full of envelopes and parcels. The children clung to his knees, chattering excitedly, trying to pull the things from his gnarled old hands, and with his usual friendly grumbles, Nickie began to distribute his mail. Those children who could read grabbed their envelopes, and hurried off into corners to open their letters, and those who couldn't tore open theirs as nurses came to read the contents to them. When all the children had at last accepted that there were no more for them, and those without letters at all had been comforted by the sweets the old man always carried for the disappointed ones, he came over to Harriet, where she was rearranging a bandage on the ear of a child who was doing his best to remove it, a large parcel still under his arm.

"There's one here I'm not sure about, Sister," he said, wheezing a little. "Delivered by hand and addressed to this ward clear enough, but it just says "Tod" on it. No last name. Who would that be, now?"

Harriet, puzzled, put her hand out for the parcel, and Nickie gave it to her. It was neatly wrapped, and the label bore the sign of a big shop Harriet knew well, a shop in the main road near the hospital. It read "Tod, c/o Sister, Children's Ward, Royal Hospital." And Harriet took it over to Tod's bed, to sit with it beside him.

"This is for you, Tod," she said gently. "Would you like to open it?" but Tod just looked at it, and made no move.

101

With a sigh, Harriet opened the parcel, and slowly began to pull out the contents.

There was a pair of brown corduroy trousers, a neat red sweater, a woollen vest and underpants, and a pair of long brown socks. Under this, there was a brown duffel coat, and a yellow woollen cap with matching mittens, and a pair of red slippers, with cowboy hats embroidered all over them. A pair of red wellington boots completed the clothes, and tucked into one of them was a small blue toy car.

There was nothing else. No letter, no card, nothing. Just the things, and the label on the wrapping. Harriet slowly began to dress Tod in the clothes, pulling the straps of the trousers up with a pin, for they were too long for the frail child, sending a nurse to get a needle and thread to make a more permanent alteration. Tod seemed uninterested, making no effort to stop her, but also not helping her to put them on. The slippers fitted well, and when she had dressed him, putting the coat, cap, mittens and boots in his empty locker, Harriet carried him to the pile of toys in the middle of the floor, sitting him down with the other children in the hope he would start playing with them. But he just sat, his legs thrust out in front of him, his face watchful.

They suit him, she thought, these clothes. And they're good ones. That's an expensive shop — but who? —

With a sudden thought, she left Tod, and tearing the label from the wrappings of the parcel, hurried to her office. With crisp movements, she dialled the number of the shop, and when they answered, asked for the manageress.

Lying with a smooth facility that surprised her, she said glibly, "I'm so sorry to bother you — but there seems to have been some sort of mistake. A parcel arrived here this morning —" she described the contents, and said then, "And this little boy doesn't know who sent them! He's the only one we have called Tod, but we wondered if there had been a mistake. May I ask if you can remember who bought them? The little boy's family would like to know if they were meant for him so that they can say thank you —"

The manageress seemed to be unsurprised, and went off to find the saleswoman who had arranged the sale, leaving Harriet clutching the 'phone with a cold hand. Maybe it was a relative, she thought with wild hope. Maybe someone does know he's here, and just doesn't want to claim him — but still wants to see he's properly equipped —

The voice of the saleswoman came clacking tinnily through the 'phone.

"Hello, Madam? You were asking about some clothes that I sold?"

Again Harriet described them, told the same lie about the child's parents, and the saleswoman seemed to accept her lies.

"Yes, I remember the sale quite well. Yesterday it was, just before we closed — it was a man bought them. He didn't seem to know the size — said the boy was about five or thereabouts. I hope the things fit all right?"

"They fit," Harriet said quickly. "Look, could you describe this man — then I can tell the child's parents —" And with a great deal of careful attention to detail, the voice described Gregory, faithfully, even remembering his voice.

"A very nice man, he was," she said cheerfully. "Money no object, you know — wanted the best. Nice of him, wasn't it? I hope the parents like the things —"

"Yes — thank you," Harriet said mechanically, and put the 'phone down as the saleswoman burbled on. She had known, really, she told herself dully. It had been mad to hope that it had been otherwise. Gregory had bought these clothes for Tod, had gone out at the end of a long day's work expressly to equip a child he swore he had never seen before in his life —

"Dr Bennett's here, Sister," a nurse's voice brought her up sharply and Harriet hurried out of her office, pulling her cuffs straight on her sleeves as she went.

Dr Bennett was standing beside the group of children in the middle of the floor, a tall man beside him, both of them looking down at Tod's still little body, an oasis of silence in the middle of the noisy group of children.

"Good morning, Sister." He greeted her with a cheerful smile. "This is Dr Jeffcoate, Psychiatrist, you know. He's come from the University to see our little mystery. I thought perhaps he'd succeed where we failed —"

The tall man nodded at Harriet, and said, "I'd like to examine this child —" and Harriet picked the unresisting Tod up, and led the way back to her office. She sat Tod on her desk, and the two men stood and looked at him, while Tod looked silently back.

Crisply, Dr Jeffcoate began to ask questions of Harriet, about Tod's behaviour, the way he ate, moved, slept, and with equal crispness, Harriet answered him.

104

She described the one occasion when Tod had seemed to respond to her, when he had slept on her lap after she had sung to him, described it in some detail. But she said nothing of what had happened the previous day.

"And he has never spoken," Dr Jeffcoate said, watching Tod.

"No," Harriet said in a low voice, almost sickened by her own lie. But she couldn't do it — couldn't possibly tell them of Gregory and Tod's recognition of him. That was something she would still have to work out for herself.

Swiftly, Dr Jeffcoate began to make a detailed neurological examination of Tod, pushing the things on Harriet's desk out of the way, and pillowing the child's head on the cushion from her chair, brusquely refusing her offer of the dressing cubicle.

"I can manage here," he said, and put out an imperious hand for an ophthalmoscope, bending to peer intently through it at Tod's blue eyes, while Tod just lay on the desk, unresponsive as ever.

Dr Bennett and Harriet watched in silence, and at last, the psychiatrist straightened, and stood looking down at Tod.

"This may be a long job," he said at length. "Whatever has happened to this child has been clearly catastrophic as far as he is concerned. It will take considerable testing and observation before I could hazard a guess at his condition or prognosis."

Dr Bennett said quickly, "We can't keep him here for much longer, Jeffcoate. Quite apart from anything else, this is a general hospital — we haven't the facilities —"

"I realise that," Dr Jeffcoate said. "I could perhaps get him a place at one of the homes I visit. And as he's a ward of court, there'll be no problems about parental consent, of course —"

"Sir," Harriet's voice sounded a little cracked as she moved forwards to stand protectively beside Tod. "Sir — may I make a suggestion?"

Dr Jeffcoate peered sharply at her under bushy eyebrows, and Dr Bennett, one eyebrow raised interrogatively, looked at her with a trace of irritation in his face.

"Well, Sister? I've told you already we can't keep him here, however attached you may have become to him —"

Beseechingly, Harriet said. "But — look, sir. The police found him near this hospital. He's too small to have wandered all that far from wherever he lived. Couldn't — couldn't I try to find his home? Just give me a little time, sir, before you move him to somewhere else. Please?"

"How do you propose to find his home?" Dr Jeffcoate asked dryly. "I gather the police have failed — how do you think you can succeed if they can't? Or have you some information we and they haven't?"

Harriet pushed her guilty memory of Tod's behaviour yesterday away, and said eagerly, "But even so, sir, no one's tried to use *Tod* to find out. Suppose — suppose he actually *saw* his home? Wouldn't he recognise it?" Of course he will, her mind said. He recognised Gregory —

"It's possible," Dr Jeffcoate said. "Remotely possible —"

"Let me try, sir," Harriet said. "Let me take him out — let me just walk him around the district and watch what happens. I know the area very well sir — I've made a point of getting to know it — and perhaps, if I'm lucky enough, I'll find a place he knows. Then — then perhaps we'll be able to discover who he belongs to —"

There was a long silence, Dr Bennett standing still, his face showing nothing, Dr Jeffcoate thinking carefully.

Then, Dr Jeffcoate said, "It will be a couple of weeks before I can arrange a vacancy in a home anyway. If you're happy about the idea, Bennett, I see no harm in it. It'll get the child out of the ward and that won't do him any harm, and there's always the possibility that Sister here is right. He could perhaps be made to respond in an environment he remembers. And once he does, of course, the problem is solved. These acute conditions rarely require intensive psychiatric treatment once the initial block is broken down."

Harriet turned and looked at Dr Bennett, her eyes pleading with him. "Please?" she breathed. "Please, sir?"

Dr Bennett cleared his throat harshly, and said, "Oh, all right, Sister. If you can find the time, and Jeffcoate is sure it will do no harm, what can I say? We can block a bed for a couple of weeks, I suppose. As it's summer, and we don't get quite so many emergency demands for beds this time of the year. But just two weeks, mind."

"Thank you, Dr Bennett," Harriet smiled brilliantly at him, and picking Tod up, held the small body close, looking at the two men over the narrow shoulders. "If I can just *try* —"

Dr Jeffcoate smiled suddenly, his face lifting out of its grim lines. "He's a lucky child, Sister. At least he's got someone to care for him. And he needs that."

And Harriet held Tod close, and said: "Yes. I care for him." She rubbed her cheeks against his smooth fair head. "I care for him."

CHAPTER
TEN

Harriet spread the map on her bedroom floor, and fixed the corners firmly with books. Then she sat back on her heels, and looked at it.

"See, Sally? If I use the hospital as a central point, and draw circles out from it, then I can map out exactly which areas to cover each time we go out. And if I really study it, then there'll be no danger of missing a single street."

Sally, lying on her front on Harriet's bed, her fair hair flopping over her face as she twisted her head to, see the map the right way up, sighed, and said, "I still think it's crazy. This hospital's in the middle of one of the most tightly packed areas of London, and you think you can cover on foot every possible place this kid could have come from. And anyway, you've no proof he even lived anywhere near here."

Patiently, Harriet went over her reasoning, point by point. "He's too small to have travelled far on foot. It is more than unlikely that any bus conductor would have let him ride on a bus by himself — even if he'd had the fare, which is equally unlikely. If he even managed to travel on the underground, why should he have chosen to come to this particular area? I know he was found near the underground station, but that was just a coincidence —"

"Hasn't it occurred to you that it's a pretty wild coincidence that he should have turned up here in the first place? I mean, if Gregory is related to him —"

"I know," Harriet said brusquely. "But maybe it isn't such a coincidence after all. I mean, if Gregory — knows — the child's mother, there'd be every reason for — for her to live near where he works —"

"Poor old Harriet," Sally said softly. "This is cutting you to ribbons, isn't it?"

"Can't be helped," Harriet said, and bent her head to her map again.

And indeed, every way she turned, the situation seemed loaded with pain for her. Convinced as she was that Tod was Gregory's son, she had been forced to face the fact that somewhere there was a girl who belonged to Gregory, belonged to him in a way she longed to belong herself. Bleakly she felt that whatever happened, even if by some miracle she and Gregory ever did build together the life she wanted, it would always be shadowed for her by the memory of this other girl. Not that it looked as though there would ever be a future now.

"He's leaving, you know," Harriet said suddenly.

Sally raised her head sharply. "Leaving? Gregory?"

"So he said," Harriet still didn't look up.

"But — he can't be," Sally said. "He's been offered the junior consultancy in urology —"

"What?" Harriet did look up now, her face blank with surprise.

"They were talking in theatre this morning," Sally explained. "Old Peter Leeman is retiring this autumn —

110

and Sir David told him that Gregory had been accepted by the Board to replace him. He didn't tell you?"

Harriet shook her head. "When did this happen?"

"Yesterday, as far as I know. Look, it's quite possible Gregory doesn't know himself yet. The Board only met last week, and you know how long it takes them to publish their mighty ponderings. I shouldn't have heard it myself — but I always eavesdrop on the surgeons' room. I can hear every word from my office, and I make sure I always do! It could be that they won't announce their decision till Founders Day, next month — old Sir David likes to bring a bit of pomp and circumstance into things, and it'd be just like him to announce the new appointment then."

"Maybe he won't leave, then," Harriet said slowly. "It's quite a thing to get an appointment like that — not even Gregory could turn it down — just because of me."

"Who knows? If he's as mixed up with his private life as he seems to be, maybe he'll be forced to give the job a miss. Face it, Harriet, for God's sake! He's supposed to be in love with you, yet it seems he's got a family of some sort already — in a mess like that, the only thing to do *is* cut and run. Quite honestly, love, it'd be best for you if he *did* leave. Give you a chance to get over him, hmm?" but Sally didn't sound too hopeful, and was forced to reply with a grin to Harriet's own rueful grimace.

"Sure," Harriet said wryly. "Gregory goes away and whoosh! All gone nasty miseries! Harriet's the same old Harriet again! I wish it were as easy as that."

Sally wisely left it there. There was little point in trying again to change Harriet's point of view. And as

Sally herself had realised, the day she had found Harriet weeping so bitterly over the little porcelain girl, somehow this love affair was meant to be. For all her practicality, Sally was aware of the inevitableness of it, the very real mutual attraction that pulled these two people together so powerfully.

So she made a pot of coffee, and sat quietly drinking hers while Harriet made a rough drawing of the area she meant to cover with Tod the next day, the first half day she had been able to arrange since Dr Bennett had given her permission to take Tod looking for a place he might remember.

She hadn't seen Gregory since that evening in the garden, when he had kissed her, a kiss she could still feel bruising her mouth if she let her thoughts take her back three days. The patients he had on her ward were either seen by his house-surgeon, or a message would come up from outpatients where Gregory would be holding a clinic, asking her to send those children he needed to see down there. There was no doubt in Harriet's mind that he was avoiding her, and much as she ached for a sight of him, to have him near enough to remind herself of the way his arms had felt about her that night that now seemed so long ago, she was obscurely grateful for his absence. In a way, she had transposed some of her feeling for Gregory to Tod, and there was one thought now that persisted above all others. She must find Tod's home. Somehow, she must find it.

It was with an absurdly optimistic lift in her heart that she got Tod dressed in his new duffel coat the next afternoon. The shoes he had been wearing the day he was admitted were polished carefully, and didn't show their shabbiness quite so badly, and she pulled the little woollen cap over his fair head, and put the mittens on his hands, even though it was summer now; he looked too fragile to be warmed even by the fitful sunshine of a typical May afternoon — typically blowy, as only an English May can be.

She had managed to beg the use of an elderly pushchair from the physiotherapy department, and she tucked Tod into it at the main gate of the hospital, and looked deeply into his eyes as she crouched in front of him, strapping his narrow body in.

"I'm going to take you for a walk, Tod, my love," she told his silent face. "Just for a walk. And if you want to go anywhere special, just show me, hmm?" But he made no movement in reply.

In later years, Harriet was to remember that first afternoon when she walked with Tod through the narrow clamorous streets of the close packed corner of London that she knew so well, remember that first afternoon in detail. She trudged up street after street, past high narrow fronted houses with flights of steps in front of them, past the blocks of flats that reared their massive bulk over the bare patches that had once been bomb-damaged during the war, threading her way through pavements filled with chattering groups of women, dodging screeching children, passing small shops, big shops, edging past patient bus queues, waiting wearily for traffic lights to change green so that they could cross the wider traffic-roaring roads.

The passing scene blurred a little, seeming to bob up and down with her own movement, and Tod's brown coated form sat slumped in the pushchair in front of her, his yellow hat bobbing too, as the pushchair went on its creaking way, the wheels squeaking their lack of oil at her.

And gradually, the circle she had planned to cover round the hospital on that first afternoon was covered. Street after street passed by them, mile after mile of grey pavement slid away under her weary feet. Three hours after she had left the hospital she began to work her way back towards it, passing along ever new roads, past rows and rows of anonymous houses. And still Tod sat still, not moving, no sign of the stiffening of the shoulders that Harriet was watching for, the sign of some sort of tension that would show her she was near his home ground.

And for a whole week, it went on. She arranged for her own off duty to be every afternoon, much to the joy of her nurses, who thus had more free evenings than they were accustomed to get. Harriet's days became a weary trek, each morning occupied with the rush of ward work, each long evening on duty ending with an exhausted bath and restless sleep, with the eternal trudging through the streets every afternoon, with Tod in his pushchair in front of her, a Tod as apparently unaware of his surroundings as he seemed to be in the ward.

Most evenings, Sally would call in at the ward on her own way off duty to ask with a mute look for news, and each time, Harriet would shake her head silently. Sally could have wept for Harriet, at the way her eyes seemed to grow larger in her face as she lost weight almost visibly, at the violet shadows that stained the hollows of her cheeks, painting the skin under her eyes with the ugly badge of fatigue. Even Paul, on his visits to patients in the ward, was worried, asking Sally privately what was the matter with Harriet — was she ill? And Sally, almost impatient at her own loyalty to what she considered Harriet's idiotic behaviour, didn't tell him, passing it off as "just one of those things".

Paul asked Harriet one evening what was the trouble, and the concern on his friendly and familiar face made the weary Harriet want to cry, to throw herself onto him, to hold onto his strength. But she had laughed with a lightness she had to fight to dissimulate, and changed the subject to a discussion of one of the children in the ward.

On each of the long afternoons when they walked through diesel smelling streets, Harriet would stop the chair for a while, would lift Tod out, and put his mittened fist on to the side of the pushchair, closing his unresisting fingers round it, so that he held on. Then, slowly she would walk on, and Tod, pulled by the chair, walked too. This at least, Harriet felt, was something. By the end of the week, he was walking more strongly, and for longer periods, before showing signs of being tired, would even begin to trot beside her if she did not make him hold on to the chair. And even as her own physical health seemed to suffer from the long and agonising programme she had set herself, so Tod seemed to improve. The food he was eating so voraciously began to show on his thin frame; he filled out, his legs losing the pathetic skinny spaghetti look, his cheeks beginning to

115

flush with the faint rose that other children had even in these crowded city streets.

As they walked, Harriet dividing her attention between the route they were taking and Tod's face, always watching for some sign that he recognised the street they were in, her thoughts would take their own way, and she was too bone tired to be able to control them.

She wondered about this girl — Tod's mother — the girl she felt sure she would find soon, one of these afternoons. For there was no doubt in her mind now that Tod had a mother, somewhere. She knew enough about children to realise that whatever had broken the bond between his mother and himself — whether it had been a street accident, or what it had been — Tod had had a close relationship with her, and it was the loss of this closeness that had driven him to the silent misery she felt in him.

She found herself weaving fantasies about the girl, fantasies that could explain her silence, explain why she had not come to find this little boy who trotted so quietly at Harriet's side. And as she grew tireder, so her fantasies became wilder, filled with melodramatic ideas of abduction, even murder. But when this happened, she forced herself to stop, telling herself with heavy common sense that the girl had probably just run off somewhere, sick of caring for her child, sick of Gregory's silence. For Harriet now believed that Gregory had wilfully abandoned the girl, the girl and her child, and had left them without a backward glance.

And so her attitude to Gregory changed, sick loathing

of him fighting the love that still filled her whenever she thought of his lean body and grizzled head, until her head spun wildly, till she hardly knew what she felt or what she was doing. Only a dumb determination to find the answer for Tod's sake kept her going.

And then, so suddenly that she was caught unawares, the very thing she had been hoping would happen did at last happen; and so tired was she that she had almost forgotten why she was walking these dreary streets with Tod.

They had just turned into a narrow alleyway of a street, a street lined on both sides with small houses whose chipped and peeling front doors opened directly onto the greasy pavements. There was no sign of any green anywhere, no front gardens to hold the dusty privet hedges that helped to liven some of the roads in the district. Only patches of bright curtains in one or two of the windows lifted the general greyness, and these were few; most of the houses were as dirty and ill kept as they were ugly.

Tod stopped short, and Harriet had walked on a few paces before she realised that the yellow hat was no longer bobbing at her side. She turned, and stared back at Tod, where he stood stock still in the middle of the pavement.

His head was up, his chin pointing straight ahead of him, his whole body rigid as his blue eyes slowly moved along the street, staring at a tiny grimy shop window full of empty packets of cigarettes and dusty models of boxes of chocolates, at the rubbish filled gutters, the narrow houses.

Almost too tense to breathe, Harriet watched him, making no sound. Then slowly, Tod began to move, to walk first, and then to run, his thin legs gathering momentum. He ran past her, without looking at her, and abandoning the pushchair, Harriet ran after him.

He stopped at the last house in the street, to stand at the front door, a door that had once been green but now bore only traces of paint on its blistered woodwork. His face had lost its stillness, the emptiness that Harriet had come to accept as part of him, was crumpled in an agonising grimace. Then, suddenly, he pushed on the door, pushed hard, and the door clicked and opened.

He stood poised in the dark opening, and Harriet stood behind him to look into the narrow hallway beyond, hardly seeing the dirty wallpaper, the unscrubbed bare wooden boards, the broken bicycle leaning against one wall.

From beyond a tattered curtain that screened the far end of the dingy hallway, a voice called "'Oo is it? That you, Joe? — 'Oo is it?" and the curtain parted. An old woman in a dirty overall, her thin hair pulled into metal curlers, a smudge of grime across her forehead, came slouching towards them, a frown appearing on her wrinkled face.

"Oo —" Then she saw Tod, and with a look of pure surprise she cried "Davey — Davey! Where you come from, Davey?"

And the child at Harriet's side screamed a loud inhuman scream, and turned to Harriet to bury his head in her skirt, to weep the first tears she had seen him weep since she had first known him.

CHAPTER
ELEVEN

He clung to Harriet, held on to her with all the strength he had, and Harriet held him close, picking him up to croon gently to him, rocking him in an attempt to soothe the bitter weeping that threatened to tear him apart.

The old woman in curlers, clucking a sympathetic counterpoint to the child's noisy weeping, pulled them both into the house, leading them into the kitchen at the end of the hallway. Even in the midst of her distress for the child who was clinging so tightly to her, Harriet was repulsed by the smell of the cluttered room, the mixture of cats, of meals long ago cooked, eaten and forgotten, of sheer dirt. The woman shoved a pile of newspapers off a shabby broken armchair, and pushed Harriet into it, and she sat and rocked monotonously, until the shaking body in her arms gradually relaxed, till the tears that stained the swollen eyes and ravaged the smooth young cheeks had stopped.

"Well, I never," the woman said, moving heavily about the tiny room, making ineffectual attempts to tidy it into some semblance of order. "What's up with him? Why's he crying so? Poor little feller — takin' it hard, is he? Well, it's no wonder, is it? Always was a quiet one, was Davey, and these quiet ones — well, they do run deep, don't they, like people always say? Quiet ones run deep."

"Look," Harriet said. "I must talk to you — but it's a bit difficult with Tod — Davey here. Is — can I 'phone from anywhere? I'll try to get him back, and then I can talk to you —"

The old woman looked dubious, and peered suspiciously at her. "Well, I don't know, I'm sure — I mean, why should you want to talk to me? From the Council are you?" She looked at the scrap of dress that showed beneath Harriet's coat, her uniform dress.

"No, I'm not from the Council. I work at the Royal — and Tod — Davey's a patient there. And I must get him back before I talk to you —"

"There's a 'phone over at the shop," the woman said unwillingly. "But I —" Awkwardly, because of the way the child was clinging to her, Harriet fumbled in her pocket, and pulled a crumpled ten shilling note out. The woman brightened, and said with senile briskness, "Well, I suppose I could go for you. 'Oo do I 'phone?"

"The Royal — and ask for Sister Andrews on the theatres. Tell her, will you, that Sister Brett needs her at once. Tell her what the address is, and tell her to take a taxi — say it's urgent."

Mutttering the message under her breath, and repeating the number to herself the old woman slouched off, and Harriet was left sitting in the dim and dirty kitchen, the child on her lap still snuffling softly as he clung to her.

Gently, Harriet disentangled his grasp, pulled him up till she could look at him. "Davey?" she said gently. "Davey?"

The child lifted his head, looked at her and repeated, "Davey," in a voice thick with tears.

"Did you live in this house, Davey, love?" Harriet asked softly. "Was this your house?"

The child nodded jerkily, and then he said, "Mummy — Mummy —"

"With Mummy?"

His face crumpled again, and tears filled the blue eyes. "Mummy —" he said, choking through his misery. "Mummy won't wake up — Mummy —"

And Harriet, unable to bear the look on his thin face held him close, letting her pity and love pour over him, too upset herself to question the pitiful little boy any more.

The woman came back very soon, and told her that she had spoken to Sally, that "She's comin' right over she says. Says not to worry — she'll be here soon as may be. Must be well off, you hospital people, takin' taxis all over the place —"

Harriet answered absently, still holding Davey close in her arms, her head full of the questions she must ask this woman, but feeling instinctively that she could not ask them in the child's hearing. Whatever had happened here was too raw, too agonising to be talked about in front of him.

The fifteen minutes that it took Sally to arrive seemed to Harriet an eternity, and her relief when she heard the door rattle, heard Sally's clear voice calling out her name was so great it almost overcame her.

She hurried to the door, carrying Davey with her, and very quickly, told Sally what had happened.

"His name is Davey — and he's desperately upset, Sally. Look, I must talk to this woman, but I can't — not till Davey's settled. Please, Sal, take him back for me, will you? Get him to bed, and get Staff Nurse to give him some nepenthe — it's written up for him and I think he needs it. I'll get on to Dr Bennett myself as soon as I get back —"

Sally nodded, and climbed back into the taxi that still sat at the curb, its engine ticking over quietly. Davey resisted at first, as Harriet gently put him onto Sally's lap.

"It's all right, love. This is Sally and she's my friend. She'll take you back to bed, and then I'll come soon. I must talk first — I won't be long —" and the child was suddenly too weary, too emotionally exhausted by his distress, to argue. Harriet watched his white face at the window as the taxi disappeared round the corner on its way back to the Royal, and then she turned, and stopping to salvage the pushchair, made her way back to the house where the slatternly woman was standing leaning against the door, chattering busily to the few women who had emerged from their own houses to watch what was going on.

"I'm sorry there was so much poise," Harries began, feeling she must propitiate this rather horrible woman if she was to get anything out of her. "But now, if you could spare the time, perhaps we could talk?"

The woman peered at her and said with a cunning sideways look at Harriet's coat pocket, "Well, time's money you know —" and obediently Harriet reached for her purse, and found another ten shilling note.

122

"Well now, Sister — Brett wasn't it?" The old woman led the way back to the dingy kitchen and settled herself in the armchair. She looked up at Harriet and grinned. "I'm Mrs Ross — owns this house I does. What can I do for you?"

"You know that little boy?" Harriet asked crisply.

"Know 'im? Know 'im? Course I do! Lived in my house two years he did! Course I know him!" Mrs Ross looked suddenly suspicious. "Any reason why I shouldn't?"

"I'd better explain —" Harriet said wearily, and as simply as she could told Mrs Ross the whole story of Tod — Davey — she would find it difficult to use his real name for some time — and the mystery that surrounded him. The woman listened enthralled, her mouth half open. "I thought I'd find somewhere he'd recognise if I tried hard enough," Harriet finished. "And he recognised this house — and that's all I know. The rest I've got to find out from you."

"Well, I never." Mrs Ross was clearly delighted. "There's a thing! Just like a film, 'nt it? Poor little sod —"

"Please," Harriet said, sickened by the look of senile pleasure in Mrs Ross's eyes. "Who is he? Where's his mother?"

"Well, that's it, you see! He's lost her — dead she is! Poor little thing!"

Slowly, Harriet got the story out of her, patiently questioning, leading the garrulous old woman back to the point every time she strayed off it, which was very often.

Davey's mother had been a girl called Susan Brooks, and she and Davey had come to Mrs Ross's house two years before. She had told Mrs Ross that her husband was dead — though Mrs Ross, with all the painfully acquired wisdom of her London background, didn't believe for one moment that she ever had a husband. Mrs Ross had let her the two top front rooms "at a shockin' low rent, mind you, but I was sorry for the poor cow —" and they had moved in. She had made her living as a dressmaker, taking in work from a small wholesale dress factory round the corner, and a very poor living it had been.

"Hardly set foot outside the place she didn't, except to fetch and carry her work. And wouldn't let the boy out neither. She wouldn't let her Davey play out in the street, not her! — kids down here not good enough, I suppose — but I'd let him play out in my back yard sometimes. She'd take him walks around the streets now and again, but not too often. And she never talked to no one, nor got a letter or anything. I told her — only a few weeks before she died, poor thing, told her she'd have to let the boy go soon. Couldn't keep him at her apron ends always, I told her. He'd have to go to school, one day — five he is, and the truant people'll be after you, I told her. But there — she just smiled the way she did, all secret, and never argued or said anything —"

"So that's why no one came forward —" Harriet said slowly.

"Eh?"

"His picture was put in the papers, and on television, but no one seemed to recognise it. If she never let him go out, no one but you really knew him well enough to recognise him —"

"In the papers, was it? Well, there! If only I'd 'a' known! But I don't take a paper — can't be bothered to read much, like — not at my age, and people like me, we can't afford no television sets —" and she leered up at Harriet greedily.

Harriet ignored the hint, and asked, "What — happened when she died?"

"Well!" Mrs Ross settled herself more comfortably in her chair, and began to talk, taking a morbid delight in her story, a delight that made Harriet's flesh creep.

Late one afternoon, Mrs Ross had gone panting upstairs to get something from the back room she used as a general junk room — she rarely climbed the stairs otherwise — and had seen Susan Brooks's door open. The other door — their bedroom door — was closed, and Mrs Ross had looked into the room they used as a living room "to say hello, like. I'm friendly, always was —" and seen the girl in a heap on the floor. In a great flurry of excitement, she had shrieked from the window to call a neighbour, and an ambulance had been called. Susan Brooks had been taken off to hospital — not the Royal, but the smaller hospital on the other side of this particular part of London, but she had been dead when she arrived there.

"Just collapsed, they said," Mrs Ross said ghoulishly, "Just up and died, the doctor reckoned. Didn't feed herself properly, he said, and then went and got this virus pneumonia. I daresay you'll understand better'n I would —"

Harriet nodded. A girl in a poor state of health could well die quite suddenly from a virus pneumonia, even after a very short illness.

"But what about Davey?" Harriet was puzzled, "Why didn't you tell anyone about him?"

Mrs Ross looked a little furtive, and glanced sideways at Harriet with hooded eyes. "Well, I never thought to, like. I mean, I wasn't to know was I? I thought as how she'd maybe sent him off to visit someone or something — I wasn't to know."

"You said she had no friends," Harriet said, cold with anger.

"Well, I wasn't to know! He wasn't here, that's all I knew. And it wasn't none of my concern. I had enough to put up with, what with her dying here like that — I wasn't going running around after a kid that's got nothing to do with me —"

"He must have found her," Harriet said, remembering the pinched little face, the way he had said, "Mummy — won't wake up —" and she felt sick. "He must have found her, and tried to rouse her, and when he couldn't, just ran out of the house in fright. No wonder he got into such a state — he must have been hurt in a traffic accident as well, and in the state of mind he was in, I'm not surprised — How could you just *do* nothing — not tell someone — the police — anyone, about him?"

"I don't go tangling with no police," the old woman said belligerently. "I told you, it was none of my concern. He wasn't my kid, was he?"

And Harriet was forced to leave it at that. How anyone could be so indolent as to do nothing in such a situation,

126

she could not for the life of her understand But so it had been and she had to accept it.

"They gave me the death certificate," Mrs Ross seemed herself to understand Harriet's anger, and began to offer more information without waiting for questions. "I couldn't do nothing about a funeral, of course — cost money, they do — but the hospital said they'd take care of that, as there was no relatives or nothing, so there you are! But I kept all her bits — well, all except for those I had to sell to get my rent — entitled to that, I was, in law —"

Harriet didn't argue, and in a cold angry silence, took the paper carrier bag the woman pulled out of a cluttered cupboard and turned to go.

"I hope you got enough rent money," she said bitterly. "It would never do if you *lost* money, would it?"

"Don't you be so high and mighty, you!" Mrs Ross flared in sudden rage. "What do you know about it? You with your taxis and your tenshillingses? You never went without in your life, did you? Well, I did, and I ain't going to again, not if I can help it. I had to clear those rooms, had to get another lodger for them — and I had every right to sell those bits. She had no one, had she? And I reckoned the boy had run off, it'd be best for him. If I'd have gone and told, they'd just have copped him and shoved him in a home somewhere — some rotten home. I reckoned he'd be better running off if that was what he'd done — better running the streets than locked up in some lousy home, poor little bastard —"

And for a moment, Harriet could understand, feel with this woman, see the reality of her dingy existence and what it had done to her. And in all fairness, her silence about Davey could have been rooted in a misguided kindness of heart. When this woman had been a child, orphans had a pretty tough time of it, she reminded herself, looking down on the dirty face peering bitterly up at her in the dull hallway. Perhaps she really meant well.

Impulsively, she put her hand out, and took Mrs Ross's gnarled one.

"I'm sorry," she said. "I think I understand. I was — upset. I've become fond of the boy, you see. Thank you for your help."

"That's all right," the woman mumbled, suddenly shy. "You wasn't to know. But like I said, when you're old, and on your own, like me, you got to take care of yourself — look after number one. No one else won't will they? I did my best for that poor cow and her bastard — and *I* like him too. He'll be all right now, won't he? You'll see after him, won't you?"

"I will," Harriet said, and left Mrs Ross standing in the door of her dirty little house, watching her as she hurried down the street towards the main road and the hospital.

Harriet turned and looked back once more, before she finally turned the corner, at the ugly little house that had been Davey's home as long as he could remember, probably, at the narrow street that had been the only place he had known. Then, with a brief wave of her hand at the distant shape of Mrs Ross, she hurried away, clutching under her arm a paper carrier bag, a bag which held all that Davey owned in the world, his inheritance from the girl who had been his mother.

CHAPTER
TWELVE

She took the paper carrier bag on duty with her, hiding it under her cape, for she had no time when she got back to the hospital to do more than put on her cap and apron and hurry on duty. And she felt that she couldn't wait till the end of the evening to look at the contents of the bag.

Tod — Davey, she reminded herself again — was sleeping the exhausted sleep of the very young when she got to the ward, and a note from Sally was waiting on her desk.

"I had to get back on duty," she had scribbled, "ran out in the middle of a list when that ghastly old woman 'phoned, so I daren't hang about. He didn't need the nepenthe, poor little scrap — he was flat out before we got back. I'll try to come to the ward as soon as I'm straight in theatre to find out what happened and apologise. I never thought it would work! If I can't get to the ward I'll see you over in the Home —"

Mechanically, Harriet worked through the evening, and when the last baby had been fed, the last visitor had left and the children were settled for the night, she almost fell into the chair at her desk. Her staff nurse, a quiet girl for whom Harriet was grateful at this moment, silently brought a tray of tea and toast, and insisted she finished all of it before consenting to go off duty.

"You look bushed, Sister," she said with some severity, "and you'll be ill if you don't eat something — you've missed your lunch every day this week," and Harriet didn't argue, drinking the tea with thirsty gratitude under the staff nurse's watchful eye.

She went eventually, leaving a junior to move quietly round the ward finishing off odd jobs before the night staff came on duty, and Harriet at last could examine the carrier bag and its contents.

She sat and looked at it for a moment, and her mind dredged up a memory of something she had read somewhere, about the death of a woman. "And all those things she didn't want seen, and all those things she didn't want touched, they were seen and touched by strangers —" and the infinite tragedy of these inanimate objects in their shabby torn container washed over her almost unbearably. And then she looked through the glass partition down the ward to where she could see bed seven with its crumpled pillow hiding Davey's fair head, and reminded herself that this was his, this bag of oddments, and that she must investigate them for him. With shaking fingers, she pulled the bag towards her, and began to pull the things out.

There were pitifully few. A cardboard box with a few pieces of cheap costume jewellery, too cheap even to have been worth Mrs Ross's attention, a needle book, a box of pins, several reels of sewing thread, a tape measure, a thimble. A writing pad and a ball point pen, a child's picture book, and a pile of photographs in an envelope completed the collection.

Harriet slowly picked up the envelope, a big brown one, and shook its contents out on to the desk. Most of them were snapshots, fuzzy blurred pictures of a fair haired girl, some taken in a garden, some on a long forgotten seaside holiday. There were a few of a child, a solemn fair baby, and peering at them, Harriet could recognise Davey's face as it had been in his infancy; even then he must have been an unhappy child, for none of the pictures showed him smiling, just staring at the camera.

And at the bottom of the pile, there was one other picture in a cheap plastic frame. Harriet turned it over, and stared at the face that looked up at her from behind the distorted clear plastic covering. It was Gregory's face, a younger Gregory, with his dark hair free of any hint of white, his face less lined than she knew it, but Gregory just the same.

She stared at it for a long time, her mind numb. So this was how Davey had recognised Gregory. This picture. The corners of the frame were scuffed with long standing on a hard surface, and Harriet thought dimly — it must have been kept where he could see it, on a table perhaps — fantasy took over again.

"Who is that, Mummy?" she seemed to hear the child's high voice asking. "That? Gregory, Davey, That's Greg." but she couldn't imagine the voice that made the answer, couldn't really visualise the girl in the photograph alive and talking to her child.

She put the picture down, and as she did, the pile of photographs slid to the floor. She bent to pick them up, and a piece of paper she had not noticed before fell out of the pile. Carefully she smoothed its grimy folds.

131

It was a birth certificate. David Weston Brooks, the firm handwriting in the section marked "Name" read. Born in the Borough of Marylebone, date of birth August seventh. Mother Susan Weston, Dressmaker. Father Timothy Brooks, Medical practitioner.

Harriet stared at it, her thoughts whirling. He's nearly six then, she thought vaguely. Too small for his age — much too small. Timothy Brooks? Who was he? And then suddenly, the full implication of the child's name hit her. David Weston Brooks. Weston. And her heart lurched sickeningly.

There was a movement behind her, and she raised eyes blurred with sudden tears to see the night nurses at the door, looking at her with faint surprise on their faces, the newly awakened look that is a night nurse's badge at the end of everyone else's day making her suddenly aware of her own deep fatigue.

With cold fingers she thrust the certificate and the photographs back into their bag, and stumbling a little over her words, gave the night nurses the report, before taking her cape and, hugging the bag close to her, slipped silently from the sleeping ward.

She stopped outside the double doors, to look stupidly at the lift waiting to take her down to the ground floor, at the porter with the pile of drums to be sterilised waiting to close the gates after her.

"I'm going down with this lot, Sister," he said cheerfully. "But there's still room for you —"

But almost without thinking, she shook her head at him, and he clashed the gates shut and rattled the lift away. Her feet seemed to move of their own volition, carrying her down one flight of stairs, along a quiet corridor, towards the doctors' quarters.

The door to the common room was half open, and she could hear a burst of laughter from the men who were sitting there over their after dinner coffee, smell the tobacco smoke that came curling through the door out into the dimly lit corridor. A maid came out of the common room, balancing a tray on one hip as she closed the door. She peered up at Harriet with some surprise, and Harriet said unevenly, "I — I was looking for Mr Weston. Is he in the common room?"

The maid looked knowingly at her, and grinned. "No, Sister. He's in his room. Always has his coffee on his own, he does. Down the end," with a jerk of her head she indicated a row of doors that ran into the shadows along the corridor, and grinned again as Harriet thanked her, and began to walk down the corridor towards the end room. Harriet could feel the girl's eyes on her back, could almost hear the unpleasant thoughts she was obviously relishing, wanted to turn and shout at her — I'm not what you think — I'm not — but she ignored her, and with a resolution she hardly knew she had, raised her hand and tapped on the wooden panels.

There was silence for a second, then his voice, a little surprised, called "Yes?"

Slowly, she turned the knob, and pushed the door open. He was sitting in an armchair, a book on his lap, the light from the small table lamp beside him throwing deep shadows on to his face. He stared at her for a long moment, then got to his feet, letting the book fall to the floor to lie ignored in a tangle of flopping pages at his

133

feet. Slowly, she closed the door behind her, and leaned against it, her heart thumping thickly under her ribs.

"Gregory —" her voice sounded harsh, croaking, and she swallowed in an effort to clear it. "Gregory —" she said again, and then went dumb, standing there, swaying a little, her eyes on his face.

He seemed to Harriet to be standing in a nimbus of light, as the lamp behind him threw his body into sharp silhouette, and when he moved sharply towards her, the whole room seemed to blur, the light suddenly shimmering redly before her eyes. It had not occurred to her that she looked anything but her usual self to Gregory, and the sudden look of anxiety that she saw on his face startled her. But to Gregory, she looked dreadful, her face devoid of any colour, her cheeks muddy, her eyes looking huge in her pinched face.

Swiftly, he pulled her forwards, leading her to the chair, taking her cape from her, and she sat still for a moment trying to push away the sudden sensation of giddiness that was making her head swim. Then, her vision cleared, and she looked at him where he sat on the edge of his bed, his hands lying loosely clasped between his knees.

"I'm — I'm sorry to come here like this," she began huskily. "I had to show you something."

She dropped her head before his steady gaze, and began to fumble in the bag she was still clutching. The big brown envelope with its pictures and Davey's birth certificate stuck for a moment almost as though it had a will of its own and didn't want to be brought out, but she

134

managed to extricate it, and wordlessly, held it out to Gregory.

There was a shadow of a frown on his face as he put out a hand to take it from her.

"Open it," she said. "Open it. It — I think it concerns you."

Slowly, he turned the envelope upside down, letting the contents fall onto the counterpane beside him, and with steady fingers, picked up the pictures one by one. She couldn't watch him, couldn't bear to see how he would react, and she closed her eyes sharply, leaning back against her chair, listening to the faint rustle of paper as he picked up the birth certificate.

The silence seemed to stretch into eternity. Slowly, she opened her eyes, blinking a little against the sharp onslaught of light.

He was sitting quite still, staring ahead of him, Davey's birth certificate in one lax hand. And then, to her sick horror, she saw the glint of tears on his lined cheeks, saw the empty misery in his dark eyes, and without thinking, she threw herself from her chair, came to crouch on the floor at his feet. He looked down at her, making no attempt to hide his tears from her, and his face crumpled at the sight of her own anxious face so close to his.

Gently, she put her arms round him, pulled his head down to rest on her breast, held him as she would a child, and he shook in her arms, trembling like a frightened baby.

How long they sat like that she didn't know. All she could think was that she had done something quite dreadful, and hurt this man she loved as no one had ever hurt him before. And then he moved, pulled himself away from her, and walked across the room to the window to stand staring out of it into the darkness.

Then his voice, thick, shaking a little with an effort to control it, came quietly across the silence.

"You had to do it, didn't you, Harriet? Had to know?"

"Yes," she said gently, suddenly feeling strong again, the weariness and misery that had beset her for so long seeming to change into a strength and a compassion she must give him. "I had to know. Not for my own sake, Gregory — not entirely. But he's so small, so lost. I have to know for him — whatever it did to you."

"Seven years ago I married Susan. Susan." His voice seemed remote, as though he were talking of someone else's marriage, not his own.

"She was twenty — eleven years younger than me. And I loved her. I'd never loved anyone before. Not till I saw her. But she — she was young, and a little spoiled, and I thought she needed me. So I married her."

"Please — don't, Gregory. Don't tell me if you don't want to. I — all that I wanted to find out was about Tod — Davey. I —"

She didn't want to listen to him, didn't want him to strip himself before her like this. It was almost indecent, as though she was an evil minded creature, as though she were sitting watching a man suffer for her own pleasure. "Don't tell me —"

"I'm going to tell you!" He whirled from the window, came to stand above her, staring at her angrily, his face harsh and ugly. "I'm going to tell you! You've done this

136

yourself — you've made me grovel, and by God, you're going to sit there and bloody well listen — and I hope you enjoy it!"

"No —" she said. "No —"

But he stood there, towering above her, making her look at him, fixing his eyes on hers.

"I loved her — but I couldn't love her as she wanted. Do you know what I mean? Do you? She wanted physical love — needed it as no woman ever needed anything — and I couldn't satisfy her. She laughed at me — taunted me. I worshipped her — wanted to cherish her, but she threw my love back at me. I wasn't a man, she said, wasn't a man. I couldn't satisfy her." He laughed suddenly, a bitter laugh. "Oh, don't look so sick! It wasn't a complete frost — I consummated our marriage, if that's what you're wondering. But I couldn't — couldn't — satisfy her. She was — voracious. She didn't want my sort of love — gentle love. She wanted —"

Harriet, her hands shaking, dropped her head into them, tried to cover her ears, "I don't want to know — don't —" but he pulled her hands away, made her listen, made her hear him.

"And then she found other people who could satisfy her — not just one — others. And when — when I tried to make love to her, she told me about them, described them — can you understand that? What it was like? Can you?"

She was crying now, tears running down her face as she shook her head at him piteously, begging him with her eyes to stop, aching at the agony in his face.

But he was remorseless. "And then she got pregnant. And the man who gave her that baby was a friend of mine — a friend. And when I told her I would go on loving her, that she would have her baby, that I would care for it, she laughed again, and told me she was sick of me, that she didn't intend to live a life with a man who couldn't please her — and she went. Just went —"

And then he stopped, sat down suddenly beside her and stared at her bleakly. Trembling, she rubbed her wet face, and looked back at him, at the brooding eyes, the tight mouth. She wanted to run, to turn and run from him, from this room, run till she could run no further. But instead, she put her hand out tentatively, closed her hand on his, and said simply. "I love you, Gregory. I love you."

It was as though a blow had come from nowhere and sent him reeling, as though an explosion had happened inside him. He seemed to crumple, to lose the bitterness that had filled his words, and his face blurred suddenly as though he would weep again.

"I know, Harriet — I know. And I love you, my own Harriet — I love you, but what can I do? How can I — what can I do?"

"Whatever happened in the past, Gregory — it doesn't matter any more. Nothing matters any more. I — I'm not as — she was. And I love you —"

He slipped back into memory, his eyes going blank as he spoke.

"I looked for her, you know, Harriet. Whatever she had done to me, she was my wife, and I looked for her. But I couldn't find her. And Brooks went away, and didn't even bother to tell me he was going. I never saw either of them again. And I looked for a long time —"

"She — she's dead, Gregory." Harriet said gently. "Dead."

He looked at her then, and his face twisted suddenly into a sick grin. "Dead? Susan? Dead?"

"Yes —" and then he began to laugh, a horrible shrill laugh, so that she shook him, put her hands on his shoulders and shook him, forcing him to stop.

"My God!" he gasped. "My God — that's funny — funny —" and he shook his head as the laughter seemed to bubble up again. "Do you know why it's funny? Shall I tell you? She left me five years ago — and in a year or so from now, it will be seven years. And do you know what that means? It means I'll be free. That I can presume her dead — that I'll be free — that I can think about you, you and me —" and he threw back his head and laughed again, laughed till tears ran down his face, till the tears began to be sobs, till he was crying in earnest, his whole body shaking with the agony of his distress.

But this last burst of feeling seemed to wring him dry. Slowly, he relaxed, relaxed in the arms Harriet had put round him again, till he was almost himself again, only the red eyes and lined face showing any sign of the storm he had gone through.

It was a long time that they sat there, she holding him close, he just lying against her, seeming to absorb strength from her. Then he moved, and sat up, running his hands through his hair, rubbing his face with still slightly shaking hands.

He stood up, and went back to stand at the window.

"Thank you, Harriet. I had no right to explode like that," he said at length, the words coming painfully.

"It's all right, my love," she said gently, and came to stand beside him. "It's all right, you know. I love you. And I'm going to marry you. Do you know that?"

But he shook his head. "No, Harriet — no. Not now. I had thought — but not now. It's — ruined. I would have told you about her when the seven years had gone — but I wouldn't have told you why — why she left me. I thought — I thought I could marry again, marry you, but I can't — not now. I couldn't let it happen again —"

"But it won't happen again —" Harriet cried. "It won't! I'm not like she was — it won't."

"But I'm the same man, Harriet. The same man who couldn't make one woman happy. And I couldn't — couldn't make you happy either — it's ruined now —"

"No — no," she began, but he shook his head at her, touched her face gently.

"I can't my love. I can't. Don't ask me to — please. I can't try again — not take a risk like that again. Don't you see? I love you — and I can't marry you. Not possibly. I can't marry you."

CHAPTER
THIRTEEN

How she got back to her room, she never knew. She had stared at his face, at his reddened eyes, and then turned and run, unable to face things any longer. It had been too much for her.

Sally had been waiting for her in her room, and at the sight of her face, had said nothing, only helping her undress, making her drink hot milk, putting her to bed as though she were a child, giving her a sleeping pill so that she drifted off into an exhausted sleep.

She went on duty the next morning with a head heavy with reaction, her face bleak and somehow old in the morning light. Her nurses looked at her in surprise, but said nothing, only working through the morning's routine with an efficiency that meant she could at least not worry about the ward, could leave things to them, and for this she was grateful. She could not have worked properly for the life of her.

The paper carrier bag with the photographs and the birth certificate was waiting on her desk for her, with a note from Gregory on top of it.

"You'll need this," he had written, in a scrawled uneven script, "They belong to Davey. I'm sorry, Harriet. I can't say more than that. I'm sorry."

She sat at her desk staring at the note for a long time. It was Dr Bennett's step behind her that pulled her back from her painful thoughts, her agonising memory of the previous evening.

He looked sharply at her drawn face, and said, "You're overdoing it, Sister. Not good. Not good."

She ignored his concern, reaching into the paper bag for the birth certificate.

"I've found out," she said baldly, and gave it to him, and he took it, and read it silently.

"Well done, Sister! I must confess, I thought you'd set yourself an impossible task — but well done —"

With a voice devoid of any emotion, she told him what had happened, what Mrs Ross had told her, and he listened with a grave face.

"Poor little devil — poor little devil," he murmured, and looked through the glass partition down the ward at bed seven, where Davey was sitting a little hunched up, staring round him at the other children, at the bustling nurses, with a flat look on his face, but at least with some apparent understanding of what was going on.

"Quite what we'll do with him now, I'm not sure," he sighed heavily. "There'll be no need to get him into a special home, not if he's managed to make some contact with us. He's more of a social problem now than a psychiatric one."

"What then? An orphanage?" Harriet asked.

"Perhaps — though it seems to me he needs a good foster home, really — loving people to take the place of his parents. I'll see the almoner, and the Children's Officer from the Council about him, and see what I can do — but there's a shocking shortage of foster homes in this district —"

With an effort, Harriet said, "A foster home? Does it have to be in this district — I mean, suppose I could find a home for him — would the Children's Officer be willing to consider it?"

"You've done quite enough, Sister — quite enough. No need for you to worry about this. I'll find an answer somehow," he said.

"But I — I've got rather fond of him," she said. "And I feel — responsible." He mayn't be Gregory's child, she thought bleakly, but he was his wife's child — and Davey has suffered enough. Someone's got to love him.

"No need —" he began again, but she interrupted him.

"I've got a sister," she said. "A vicar's wife. They live in Devonshire, in a huge old house, and they've got three children of their own — as well as foster children — and I think she'd be happy to have him —"

"I must say it sounds eminently suitable —" he said after a moment. "Have you already suggested this to her?"

"No, but I could 'phone — and I know Sybil will be glad to have him. She loves children, and she's the sort of girl who wouldn't be able to let him go on unwanted like this —"

"Well —" He thought for a while, then he said briskly, "I must say it would solve the problem very nicely. We've got to get him out of here soon. He's physically fit, and we need the bed. Talk to your sister, then, and I'll discuss the matter with the powers-that-be this morning —" He turned to go, but Harriet put a hand out to stop him.

"Please — Dr Bennett — someone will have to tell him, tell Davey — about his mother. That she's dead. And —" she drew a shuddering breath, "I don't think I can do it. I can't — I'm probably the best person to tell him, I know. I've spent more time with him than anyone else, but I can't do it —"

He looked down at her unhappy face, at the pleading eyes, and smiled gently.

"All right, Sister. I'll tell him. It might be better, at that. I'm less emotionally involved than you are —"

She watched him as he went down the ward, his tall figure stooping slightly, saw him stop beside Davey, talk to him for a moment, saw Davey look up at him, saw his lips move as he spoke in answer.

Dr Bennett bent, and picked him up, carrying him out to the sunny balcony, empty yet of children, most of whom were still finishing their breakfasts. I hope he manages to help Davey understand, she thought bleakly. But it will be a long time before he really gets over this. Poor Davey. Poor baby.

She reached for the 'phone, and asked the switchboard operator to make a person to person call to Sybil, promising to come down later to sign for the cost of the call, and sat with the 'phone to her ear as she waited for the connection, listening to the clicks and the distant voices of operators as the long miles to Devonshire were covered.

Sybil's voice sounded distant, but warm and friendly as always, and for a moment, Harriet could hardly speak in answer to her "Hello? Hello?" so suddenly lonely did she feel, so suddenly yearning to be there with her, to see her plump happy face, hug her close.

"Sybil?" she managed at last. "Sybil darling? It's Harriet —"

"What's the matter?" She could hear the anxiety, the rush of fear that Sybil felt at the sound of her strained voice.

"It's all right — but I need your help. And you said to ask when I needed —" As quickly as she could, Harriet told her about Davey, told her of his need for a foster home, and finished awkwardly, "He's — he's more than just a patient to me, Sybil. He — he's connected to someone — someone I know. I can't explain now, but I will."

"Of course we'll have him, Hattie," Sybil's voice came quickly. "Of course we will — as soon as you like. He can share Jeremy's room — Jeremy's the same age, and he loves company. As soon as you like —"

"Bless you, Sybil. I — I'll phone again as soon as I know what the arrangements are — we'll have to get permission from the Children's officer —"

"It'll be all right," Sybil said reassuringly. "We've fostered children before, remember — we're registered foster parents. Tell them that — they can check with the Children's Officer at Exeter — it'll be all right —"

After that, things moved quickly. Dr Bennett came back to the office, after settling Davey in bed again, and writing up a mild tranquilliser for him. "It'll help a little," he told Harriet as he signed the prescription sheet. "He took it well — too well. Too quietly. He'll have a storm about it all some time, and this will help him when it happens —"

There was a great deal of telephoning, between the hospital and the Children's officer, the police and the Court official who was responsible for Davey, the Children's Officer in Exeter, and Sybil and Edward in their distant vicarage, but by lunch time, the whole thing was settled. Davey was to go to Devonshire two days later.

Dr Bennett came back to the ward in the early afternoon to see Harriet and tell her what had been finally arranged.

"I've been talking to Matron," he told her, "and asked her if she can spare you to take the child to his new home yourself. You're the best person, and the break won't do you any harm. And she's got a Sister to replace you for a few days, so it's settled. And I've told her you've been overworking —" he silenced Harriet's protest with a raised hand, "and she's sending the replacement for this afternoon. You take the rest of today off, Sister — I insist."

Harriet didn't want to go off duty in the least. Without the ward to keep her mind occupied, she would have too much opportunity to think, to remember Gregory's unhappiness, to think about a future without him, for it was obvious that he had meant what he said. That he couldn't marry her, love her though he did. But she was too weary to argue, and she trailed off, leaving a cheerful junior Sister in charge, to make her way heavily across the crowded courtyard, weaving her way past ambulances and hurrying medical students, and outpatients searching for various departments where they had been sent for special tests, towards the Home.

But before she could reach the gate to the garden, hurrying footsteps behind her caught her up, and a hand on her shoulder pulled her back.

"Harriet — what's the matter? Are you ill? You look ghastly —"

She looked up at Paul, at his handsome face, at the eyes full of concern, and shook her head. "It's nothing —" she began. "Nothing —" and then, to her horror, her eyes brimmed with tears, and her jaw shook so that she couldn't speak, and with a shake of her head, she turned and tried to run away from him.

But he fell into step beside her, followed her through the gate into the garden, and made her stop and sit down on one of the benches under the trees.

He put an arm round her shoulder, and after a moment's resistance, she relaxed, drooped against him, and let the tears run unheeded down her face. He said nothing, just held her, letting the tears fall, mopping gently at her face with a big white handkerchief that smelled faintly of antiseptic and tobacco.

Gradually, she stopped crying, and managed to sit straight again, taking the handkerchief to blow her nose, setting her cap straight on her head.

"What is it, Harriet? What's happened? Tell me, love. This is Paul, remember?"

She looked up at him, at the crinkled eyes looking at her with so much affection, at the broad shoulders, the square jaw, and drew a shuddering breath.

"Yes —" she said, "I remember —"

I loved him once, she thought. Not as I love Gregory, but I loved him. He's comfortable, and he's fun, and he loves me.

Her voice came to her as a surprise, as though it were someone else's.

"Paul — do you still — care for me? A little?"

He looked down at her, and his mouth twisted a little wryly.

"I may be pretty volatile, Harriet, but I'm not that volatile. Yes, I love you. Very much indeed. Does it matter?"

She managed a smile then. "It matters. I — need loving, just now. Need it a great deal —"

"What's happened, Harriet? Has — what has Weston done to you? Is — is it what I thought? Is he married?"

"No," she shook her head. It's not a lie, she told herself a little defensively. Not a lie. Susan is dead, and he isn't married any more.

"What then?" Paul persisted.

"It — circumstances," she shrugged a little. "Things can't always be the way you want them to be. Circumstances — alter things. It — oh, it's such a mess, Paul! Such a mess. And I'm lost — lost and miserable, and I need loving so much —"

His face went blank, and she felt his arm round her shoulder slacken.

"I see," his voice was flat. "I see. You still love him, don't you, Harriet? Circumstances haven't changed that, have they? You love Weston?"

She sat very still for a long moment, then she said slowly. "Yes — I do — I do. It's not like a — a tap. I can't just turn it off because I want to. But I wish I could — my God, I wish I could!" She looked up at him then, tried to smile. "But it will change, Paul. It must. I — I can't go on like this —"

He rubbed his face, running his fingers through his hair, looking at her with indecision in his eyes.

"You — are you trying to tell me it's finished, Harriet? That you won't be seeing him again?"

Bleakly, she nodded. "Yes," she said. "It's finished. It's got to be — I can't cope any more —"

"Harriet —" his voice seemed to be pulled from him. "You asked me if I still cared for you. And I said I did, and I mean it. But — but I can't just pick things up where we left off. I love you — too much for that. Can you understand that, Harriet? I'll always care for you — not always as now, perhaps, not always with a — with a pain. But I always will care. But it's too late, Harriet —"

"Too late?" she stared at him stupidly.

"I wanted to marry you, once, Harriet — wanted it more than anything in the world. But what I want from marriage, what I've got to give — we couldn't have together, not now. Whatever has happened between you and Weston has — spoiled things. I'd never be able to make you happy now, Harriet. And — and you couldn't make me happy. He'd always be there, you see. I — I could never be sure I wasn't second best, never be certain you'd married me because I was me, or whether I was just — just a bolthole for you. And I'm not the sort of man to settle for second best. Even with you. Forgive me, Harriet, and try to understand. I do love you — if you can believe that. But it's too late —"

She closed her eyes against the sick pain in her, against the surge of hurt that welled up, and nodded heavily.

"I — forgive me, Paul," she said "Forgive me. I — it was an insult. I should have known better. But — you caught me at a bad moment. I hadn't had time to think. Forgive me."

He put his hand out impulsively, tried to take hers, but she pulled back. "Oh, God, Harriet — maybe I'm wrong? — I don't know. Maybe it isn't too late? —"

But she stood up, pulling her cape around her.

"No, Paul. You were right the first time. It is too late. Goodbye, Paul —" she stood for a second looking down at him, at his unhappy face and slumped shoulders, then touched his cheek gently. "Goodbye, Paul —" she said gently. "Be happy my dear."

And she turned and went, ran across the garden to the Home, leaving him sitting in the bright May sunshine, his hair blowing a little in the morning breeze, sitting still on a bench under a green tree.

CHAPTER
FOURTEEN

Sally came to her room at lunchtime, peering anxiously round the door to see her lying on her bed, still in uniform, as she had lain ever since she had left Paul in the garden.

Sally pushed her to one side and sat beside her to look down at the white face on the counterpane with a thin smile.

"Well?" she said.

Harriet looked at her, and managed a smile herself.

"Well," she repeated.

"So, what's happened? Have you see Gregory about Tod — I mean, Davey?"

Harriet nodded bleakly. "I've seen him," she said, and told Sally everything, past thinking about her pride, past anything, except the need to pour out her distress at someone's feet. And she told her why Gregory had asked her to wait, what had happened to his marriage with Davey's mother.

Sally listened in silence, and when Harriet stopped talking, stirred slightly, reaching in her pocket for a packet of cigarettes.

"I think I can understand up to a point," she said slowly, watching the thin grey smoke curling from the cigarette she lit. "Once the seven years were up, once he could feel free, he'd have been able to start — fresh — again. But why give up now? I mean, he *is* free — really free. Even after the seven years were up, even if the court had presumed her dead and said he was free to marry again, there would have been a chance she'd turn up again. But this way, it's all right. She's dead."

"I — think it's because I've found out by myself." Harriet said painfully. "I've become involved with Susan, this way. So I'm as much a part of his misery over her, as much a part of his sense of failure with her as — as she was herself. He wants no part of me now because I'm tied up with Susan in his mind, and — and he feels he won't be able to make me happy because he couldn't make her happy."

"For God's sake, Harriet! What's the matter with the man?" Sally said irritably. "All right — so his first wife was nearly a nymphomaniac — does that mean every other woman is, that you are?"

"Don't —" Harriet closed her eyes, tried to close her ears against Sally. "Don't —"

"Mincing words doesn't help," Sally said briskly. "That's what she was, wasn't she? Admit it — and Gregory should admit it too —" she stopped short, and then said wonderingly. "There's one odd thing, you know."

"What?" Harriet muttered, not caring much.

"Well, if she was — like that — why did she live as she did these last years? You say Mrs Ross told you she had no friends — never went anywhere. It doesn't sound very logical, does it? She wasn't the sort of woman to live the life of a celibate —"

"Christ, don't ask me," Harriet said with sudden violence. "How can I know? How can anyone know? Perhaps it was because of Davey that she changed, perhaps because this other man — Brooks — left her in the cart. Who knows? She might have loved Brooks — might have changed because he abandoned her. No one will ever know — and I don't want to. I don't want to think about her again."

There was a long silence, then Sally said, "What happens now? About Davey?"

"He's going down to Devonshire — Sybil's going to foster him."

"Good for Sybil. Does she know about the story?"

"Not yet. I'm taking him down there the day after tomorrow. I'll tell her then."

"And what about Gregory? I mean, is he going to — to take any interest in the child? He must be concerned about him. Why else did he buy those clothes?"

Harriet shrugged. "I don't know. I didn't even mention the business of the clothes to him when I talked to him last night. There's no — legal reason for him to be concerned. The child isn't his —"

"No — but he is his wife's child."

"I — I suppose I'll have to ask him. I haven't told them — Dr Bennett, or the Children's Officer — about the relationship between Gregory and Davey's mother, and there's no reason why I should, or why they'd ever find out. Even though she gave Davey the second name of Weston, it's not too uncommon a name. No reason why anyone should ever connect Gregory with the whole mess at all."

"But you'll talk to him about it?" Sally persisted.

"I'll — I'll probably write a letter. It'll be easier that way. He — said last night he — wouldn't see me again. I suppose he'll refuse that job here, and go on somewhere else."

"Always on the run," Sally said softly, and stood up. "What about you, now, Harriet? What will you do?"

Harriet sat up, and ran her fingers through her tousled hair. "I haven't thought about it yet," she said wearily. "Stay on here, I suppose. I've got a good job — and friends," she smiled up tremulously at Sally, "and I'll settle for that."

"There's still Paul —" Sally began, but Harriet shook her head violently. "No — not any more. I — I'll tell you about that some time — not now. I'm too tired, Sal. But Paul is — finished with me."

And wisely, Sally said no more.

Harriet slept for most of the remainder of the day, tossing heavily, later to lie awake for the greater part of the night, her thoughts chasing each other through her head with sick monotony. But she was beyond constructive thought, unable to see her way clear, however hard she tried.

"I'll see Davey settled," she promised herself in the cold light of dawn, when she got up, finally giving up any attempts at more sleep. "I'll see Davey settled, and then just — see what happens."

She spent the next day on duty working with automatic precision, going through the motions of showing

154

interest in what she was doing, grateful that Davey slept for most of the day, removed from stress as he was by the tranquillising drugs Dr Bennett had ordered for him. She took no off duty that day, staying in her office to make lists and write down all the information the relief sister would need to run the ward during her absence in Devonshire. She sent most of the nurses off duty early, leaving the ward to the care of herself and one junior as the day came to a weary end at last.

It was half an hour before the night staff were due on duty, when she was sitting beside the bed of one restless child who had had an eye operation that day, that the 'phone rang shrilly in her office. The junior hurried to answer it, and came out to Harriet breathlessly when she had hung up.

"There's a child coming up from Cas, Sister," she reported importantly. "Sister there says he's got a — a laryngeal obstruction — and could you get a steam tent ready for him, and Mr Weston'll be up to see him right away —"

As she hurriedly prepared a cubicle for the emergency, sending the junior to get steam kettles, arranging the bed and the tent, checking oxygen cylinders, Harriet found her hands shaking. She had forgotten the possibility that they would meet on duty like this, but she reminded herself that this *was* work, that this child on his way would be the only point of contact between them. There would be no need for any personal talk, she told herself, almost in panic.

The big double doors swung open, and the trolley from Casualty came through it, a porter at the foot,

Gregory at the head, holding onto the child on it. Harriet could hear the harsh whooping of the child's breathing, could see the red blankets that covered him heaving as the small body struggled for breath. With the smooth speed of long practice, she helped the porter bring the trolley to the side of the bed in the prepared cubicle, gently helped Gregory lift the child on to the bed, and stood for a moment looking down at the face on the white pillows. His grey eyes were staring, tears running from them, down the grimacing face to the drawn back lips, lips blue with lack of oxygen, and his brown hair was sticking to the sweating forehead in pathetic wisps.

Together, she and Gregory straightened the straining body in the bed, arranged the steam kettles so that the tent of sheets that had been erected over the head of the cot filled with the damp greyness of steam.

But it made no difference. The horrible whooping went on, the harsh sound of air struggling to pass whatever obstruction was nearly closing his air passages filling the small cubicle with sound, so that Harriet felt her own lungs constrict, seemed to feel as though she were herself choking, found herself breathing deeply in an impotent effort to breathe for the ill child in the steam tent.

"It can't be an infective oedema —" Gregory muttered. "I haven't been able to look properly — the child's too ill. It must be a foreign body —"

"Tracheotomy?" Harriet asked quickly, and Gregory nodded.

She flew to the sterilising room, to grab the tray that was always ready set up for just such emergencies as

156

these, and hurried back up the ward to the cubicle as though all the hounds of hell were after her.

Gregory was bending over the child, his face white, and for a moment Harriet couldn't think what had happened. Then, she realised. The sound had stopped. The whooping that had filled their ears had gone, and the child was stretched rigid on the bed, his eyes wide, his face an ominous blue.

"It must have moved," Gregory said desperately. "The obstruction's complete — I only hope it's above laryngeal level —"

Swiftly, Harriet shoved the sandbag that was part of the tray she was carrying under the thin neck, a neck now rigid with engorged blood vessels, and held onto the child's shoulders as Gregory pulled the cover from the tray, and grabbed the gleaming scalpel that lay nested in a piece of gauze on it.

"Here goes," he muttered, and with steady fingers, gently set the edge of the knife on the blue skin at the base of the throat. Smoothly, he put pressure on the knife, and the edge split the straining skin so that it parted, probed deeper, opening a channel straight into the child's windpipe.

Blood oozed onto the skin, running in purplish streaks down over Harriet's hands on the small shoulders, and then, as Harriet and Gregory held their own breaths in agonising tension, there was a hissing whistle as the air entered the small incision.

"Thank God," he said. "Thank God — it's above laryngeal level —" and he reached for the narrow silver tube on the tray. Gently he eased the curving section of

157

the tracheotomy tube into the incision, and pushed the inner tube in, making a clear hole through which air could enter. And slowly, the child's face lost its blueness, slowly the narrow chest began to heave as the lungs again filled and emptied with air.

With fingers shaking a little, Harriet threaded tapes through the narrow slits at the edge of the tube, tied them carefully round the thin neck, arranged gauze under the edges so that the delicate skin wouldn't be hurt by the rigid metal, and then straightened her back to look down on the child.

His eyes were closed now, his face smooth again, the look of fear gone as his body greedily took in air, his skin gradually showing a more normal colour.

There was a soft rattle at the door as an anaesthetist came in, pulling his big anaesthetic machine behind him.

"Casualty told me about this kid." His voice sounded oddly loud in the small room. "What gives, Weston?"

"Foreign body," Gregory said crisply. "I've done a tracheotomy. You're a bit late —"

The anaesthetist grinned cheerfully. "Wouldn't you know it? Dragged this thing right from the theatres like a carthorse, and now you don't want it —"

"Yes I do," Gregory said with decision. "I'm going to find this obstruction right now and get it out before it moves any further. You game?"

"Sure —" The anaesthetist pulled his machine to the side of the bed, and began to check the cylinders. "Fire away —"

"Got the gear, Sister?" Gregory didn't look at her, turning instead to the washbasin in the corner to scrub his hands.

158

"Yes sir," Harriet said. "I'll get it —"

As she rapidly laid a trolley in the sterilising room, putting out the special long forceps that would be needed, the mouthgag and tongue holders, Harriet found her head spinning, a combination of fatigue and tension making her whole body ache. But she pushed the trolley into the cubicle with strong arms, scrubbed her own hands steadily as the anaesthetist carefully connected his anaesthetic tubing to the tracheostomy tube in the child's throat.

"He's ready," the anaesthetist's voice seemed to Harriet to come from a great distance, as she stood beside the bed, facing Gregory across it.

"Right." Carefully, Gregory set a mouthgag in position, holding the child's jaws wide, clipped the tongue holders on, jerking his head at Harriet to take the handle from him, to keep the tongue out of the way as he worked.

Then he went behind the bed, to bend forward to peer deep into the child's mouth, gently easing the blade of the big laryngoscope Harriet gave him with her other hand into the small throat. The little bulb on the laryngoscope lit the mouth redly, gleaming on the small milk teeth, and then Gregory grunted in satisfaction.

"I can see it — forceps, Sister —"

She slapped the long handled forceps into his hand, and moving his fingers with the careful precision of a machine, Gregory probed, tensely clipping the forceps closed on the still invisible object that was blocking the child's larynx.

"Got it!" he said triumphantly, and carefully eased the forceps up and out.

159

"A marble!" the anaesthetist peered at it, and laughed loudly.

"Little devil — a marble! And a king marble at that!"

The big round marble glinted gaily in the teeth of the forceps, the light swirling prettily on the gaudy red and blue glass, and Harriet laughed shakily too.

"They will do it," she said, her voice cracking a little. "They will do it —"

Gregory's voice seemed to come from a great distance as the light in the cubicle began to swirl in front of Harriet's eyes just as the gaily coloured marble had swirled before.

"I'll leave the tracheotomy patient for tonight, Sister — there'll probably be oedema, and we don't want to take any chances. Give him a massive dose of penicillin to avoid any sepsis, and I'll see about closing the incision in the morning. He'll need a special nurse, and frequent suction on the tracheotomy tube —"

"They will do it," Harriet said again stupidly. "Tell children not to put things in their mouths, and they will do it — marbles are dangerous — they will do it —"

And then the light swirled more brightly than ever reddening in sickening circles to disappear in a grateful black wave.

CHAPTER
FIFTEEN

When she opened her eyes, she was lying on the couch in the dressing cubicle, and she stared round her stupidly, plucking at her collar which was open, aware of the looseness of her belt, which someone had undone.

"The child —" she said, suddenly remembering. "The child —" and she tried to sit up.

"It's all right," Gregory's voice pulled her eyes round, to where he was standing at the head of the couch. "The night staff are here, so you're off duty now. He's all right —"

She sat up, her head still spinning a little. "I'm sorry," she said. "I beg your pardon. I — can't think what happened —"

"You fainted." His voice was strained. "Have you been eating properly?"

"I —" she looked up at him, and then dropped her eyes. "No — I suppose not. Stupid of me."

"I haven't been eating much either." He said, and came round the couch to sit beside her. "Harriet — this was my fault, wasn't it?"

"Yours?" she looked at him, pulled her body away from the nearness of his, suddenly wanting to get away. "No — not really."

"I've made you unhappy — more than unhappy. Ill. You look — ghastly."

She managed a smile at that. "You're looking pretty grim yourself," she said huskily. And indeed he did, his face seeming more heavily lined than ever, his eyes grim in shadowed sockets.

"I've been trying to think," he said heavily. "Trying to make some sense out of this mess, but it's no use. I can't. You — you're the best thing that ever happened to me, but I'm afraid — afraid to hold onto you. I can't believe that we could ever —" He stopped, seeming to struggle to find words. "Already, I've done this to you — made you look ill, made you so miserable you forget to eat, so that you faint —"

"I'll get over it," she said, pulling the shreds of her pride round her. "I'll get over it —"

There was a long silence. Then he said heavily. "I'm right, aren't I? It wouldn't work for us, Harriet. I'm no use to you, any more than to myself. If I thought I had it in me to make you happy, to be the sort of — of husband you deserve, I — I can't tell you what it would mean to me. But I know I couldn't. It's finished, Susan — destroyed me."

She looked at him, at the face she cared for so much that it hurt, and said gently. "You're making too much of this, Gregory. Far too much. It would take more than a Susan to destroy you, whatever you think now. She's hurt you — hurt you dreadfully, but you could recover —"

He shook his head, getting up to walk restlessly about the room. "I can't take the chance. I can't — not when it's you that will suffer. If I married you, and — failed to —"

"God Almighty, Gregory!" Suddenly she was angry, wanted to shake him, locked in a fury that pulled her from the couch to stand swaying a little beside it. "Is that all you think a marriage is? Just sex? Do you think that that's all I need from marriage? A — a mate, as though I were an animal? If I *were* like that — if I needed sex so desperately, don't you think I'd have found it out about myself before now? I'm twenty five years old, remember? Would I still — still be the virgin I am if I was the same sort of woman Susan was? I know sex matters, but it's not the only thing! Doesn't respect, companionship, simple love, have any place? What do you think I am, for Christ's sake? I'm a woman that loves you — and it's *all* of you I want — not just the — the sexual satisfaction you seem to care about so much!"

He came to stand beside her, to hold her face between cold hands.

"Dear Harriet," he said softly. "Dear Harriet. How can you know? How can you? I felt like that once — before Susan. But I know now, as you can't possibly, just how important it is. When you love someone really love them, sex *does* matter. It mayn't be the only thing — but if that goes wrong, it poisons everything else. Companionship and love and friendship — none of them matter when you can't — express what you feel properly. I saw what the failure of sex did to Susan — and I'm not going to let it happen to you. There'll be someone else for you, Harriet. Someone else will make you happy as I never could. Try to believe me."

She looked up at him, and her heart seemed to fill with defeat. There was no answer she could make, no argument she could set against the flatness of his eyes, nothing she could do to convince him he was wrong.

And then, almost against her will, thought welled up in her, thoughts that showed her the one argument she could make, the only way she could show him he was wrong.

"All right," she said, pulling away from him, turning to the glass fronted instrument cupboard to use it as a mirror as she fastened her collar, and straightened her crumpled uniform. "All right, Gregory. I'll try to believe you," and her voice sounded cool and composed.

"Thank you, Harriet," he said. "That's all I ever seem to say to you, isn't it? But I mean it —"

Without turning she said, "I'm taking Davey down to Devonshire tomorrow. My sister is going to foster him. I know he's not — not your child, but you are — connected to him. It's only fair that Sybil should know the whole story, don't you think? If she's to help him as he should be helped? Could you — could you come down too, meet her, help me explain to her?"

He stood very still, and then said. "I see. Tomorrow, you say?"

"Yes."

"I — I suppose I owe him that at least. Whatever happened, it was none of his doing. I'll — I'll get someone to stand in for me for a couple of days."

"We're taking the ten o'clock train from Paddington," she said, and turned to look at him. "Will you travel with us?"

He nodded. "Yes," he said. "I'll be there," and he put a hand out towards her, an odd look of appeal on his face, but then dropped it, and turned and went.

Harriet went off duty in a sort of dream, her head filled with only one thought. As she packed a case with the few things she would need in Devonshire, as she bathed and got ready for bed, that thought went round and round.

"If he thinks that sex is all that matters, I'll show him. Prove to him he needn't be afraid. I'll show him —"

But even as she thought, her mind refused to go further. Quite how she would show him, as she put it, she wasn't sure. But she would. Somehow, in the peace of the country, away from London and all the memories of Susan that London held for Gregory, she would show him.

She sat in the window of her bedroom, the room she always had when she stayed with Sybil, staring out at the garden, letting the warm peace that was so much a part of this house wash over her. She could smell the warm drift of flowers from below, see the faint glimmer of white from the big bed of cottage pinks under her window, and she closed her eyes gratefully.

It had been a long day, and she could still feel the sway and rattle of the train journey in her bones, almost smell the oily dusty reek of the long rushing over the miles, still feel the weight of Davey on her lap, as he had sat there all through the long hours, refusing to move from her arms.

Gregory had sat beside her throughout, speaking only of commonplaces, getting food for them from the restaurant car, because Davey seemed to panic at any suggestion that they move from their compartment, helping her feed him, wrapping a rug round him when he fell asleep on her lap afterwards.

Sybil and Edward had met them, Sybil clucking over Davey in a way that seemed to reassure him, so that he had gone to her without demur, allowing her to bath him and put him to bed in Jeremy's room, falling into an exhausted sleep as soon as his head touched the pillow.

And after the children had gone to bed, the four adults sat long over their belated supper, while painfully, Gregory told Sybil and Edward about Davey, leaving out as much as he could about his own relationship with Susan, about the causes of the failure of their marriage.

Edward had said little, only listening, but Harriet felt that he knew somehow, understood what lay behind Gregory's halting words, felt his eyes on her own bent head, aware of the sympathy and affection in them.

And now, the day was over. Sybil and Edward had gone to bed, Sybil hugging Harriet warmly as she went, saying nothing, just holding her close in a sympathetic lovingness that brought tears to Harriet's weary eyes. And Gregory had said goodnight stiffly, and gone up to his own room at the other side of the house, avoiding looking at Harriet, including her in his impersonal politeness.

She opened her eyes and looked round at her room, a room that was home to her. The furniture sat shadowed in the darkness, comfortable and shabby, and the narrow bed with its patched cover looked inviting. For a moment, she wanted just to run to it, to bury her head under the covers, and fall into the oblivion of sleep.

But Gregory was going back to London tomorrow. Tomorrow. If she was to make any effort to hold him, to convince him there was a future for them together, now was the last time she could make that effort. After tonight, it would truly be too late.

She stood up, suddenly cold, pulling her thin nylon nightgown round her, and with a lifted head, moved across the room to pick up her cotton housecoat. As she put it on, she shivered, painfully aware of its flimsiness.

"I can't," she thought with sudden panic. "I can't — not me — I'm not like this really. I'm not — I can't —" But part of her mind said with cold repetition, "You must. It's the only way. You must —"

The door creaked slightly as she pushed it open, and slipped out into the dimly lit hall, and she stood poised in sick fear, waiting for Sybil and Edward's door to open, desperately trying to think what she would say if they did come out to see why she was prowling about in the silence of the night. But there was no movement, no sound but her own uneven breathing.

Her slippers moved softly over the carpet, as she walked along the wide hallway towards the blank door at the far end, and she tried desperately to control her uneven breathing, tried to stop her legs shaking against the folds of her thin nightdress.

It was as though she were someone else, a tiny Harriet perched high in the corner of the hall, looking down in sick disgust at the figure standing in front of Gregory's silent door.

"What are you?" this small Harriet jeered from her distant place. "What are you? Are you going to make a fool of yourself — at best, a fool of yourself? Or will you be able to do this? Can you crawl to this man, beg him to make love to you, be the sort of woman who cares so little for her own self respect — can you?"

"I must," she thought desperately. "I must. It's the only answer — I must —"

She pushed the door open, stepped inside, and closed it behind her to lean against the panels in numb terror.

The curtains were wide open, moving gently in the breeze from the open window, and the light of a late moon filled the room with a dim radiance. He was lying in bed, his hands clasped behind his head, his eyes staring at the window, and he moved sharply as the door closed behind her.

He reached out, and switched on the small bedside light, so that the moonlight disappeared in a rush of yellow light that made her blink.

"Turn it off," she said breathlessly. "God, turn it off —"

After a long moment when he stared at her, he did turn it off, and Harriet breathed deeply in the grateful darkness.

She could hear the soft rustle as he got out of bed, pulled his dressing gown across his shoulders.

Then, with a last burst of resolution, she crossed the room, came to stand beside him, close to him, looking up at his face shadowed in the soft moonlight.

"Gregory —" she could feel the warmth of his body close to hers, could feel the rise and fall of his chest as he breathed, and she moved closer, putting her cold arms around his neck.

"Gregory, I love you — I love you. I need you, Gregory. Don't send me away — don't — please —"

She couldn't believe this was herself, that this woman straining her body so close to the rigid one she held in her arms was Harriet, that she could possibly be behaving like this.

"Don't send me away," she whispered again, and put her face up, seeking his mouth with cold lips, pulling his head down into a long kiss.

For a moment he resisted, pulling back from her, rigid with control. Then it was as though a wall had fallen, had burst in her arms, and he was holding her close, kissing her with a violence she couldn't have believed was in him.

"Harriet — Harriet," he murmured at last, lifting his head to look at her. "My Harriet —"

And then he was kissing her again, holding her in a grasp that seemed to melt her bones, pulling her against him, so that they fell against the bed, till they were lying locked together in an embrace that seemed to Harriet to last an eternity.

And then she knew, knew she was right. She could feel the passion in him, feel the urgency of his whole body as he held her close, as his hands moved on her cold skin in desperate caresses that made her tremble in answering need, that made her body shiver with sensations she could not have imagined possible.

"Harriet," he said again and again, the sound of his voice a caress, full of a longing that every fibre of her answered.

And then, suddenly, the curtain at the window moved again, rustling softly against the sill, and it was as though she were pulled out of herself, pulled out of her body to think logically again, to be the person she always was.

She was aware of every detail about her, of her slippers where they had fallen from her feet onto the floor, of the tumbled bedclothes under her, of the way his hair showed tousled against the brightness of the window, of the furniture seeming to stare at her with watchful eyes.

And with every ounce of strength she had, she pulled back from him, away from his arms and urgently caressing hands, to huddle crouched against the door trying to pull her dressing gown around her.

"What am I doing? My God, what am I doing?" she said in a wondering voice. "What am I doing? —" and then she was crying, shaking against the door in an agony of shame and fear, her head down so that her hair fell against her cheeks to stick against their wetness in wispy strands.

He was very still, half lying on the bed, staring across the dim room at her huddled figure, his body seeming to shake in answer to her own trembling.

Then he was beside her, picking her up like a child, cradling her in his arms, rocking her gently as he murmured in her ears.

"It's all right, my darling — it's all right — hush, my love, hush —"

Gently he crossed the room, to sit in the deep armchair by the window, holding her on his lap, her head against his chest, soothing her gently.

"I — I wanted — I wanted to show you," she began at last in a thick whisper as her tears stopped. "I had to show you you were wrong, but I can't — I can't do it — I love you so, but I can't."

"It's all right, my darling," he said again, and there was an exultant lilt in his voice, as he held her close again, rested his cheek against hers. "It's all right —"

She pulled away from him, to peer into his face in the dimness, and her voice was full of appeal, when she spoke.

"I'm not — I'm not really like this, Gregory. Truly I'm not. But I love you, Gregory — I love you. I couldn't bear to lose you, I had to show you —"

"Harriet, my own love," he said, his voice full of a tenderness she had never heard before. "I know — I know what you are — what sort of person you are. I know just how hard it must have been for you to do this — to come to me like this — and oh, Harriet, you can never know how wise you were —"

He put his head down and kissed her, a long gentle kiss that made her shiver and then relax, that filled her with a peace as unlike the passion she had felt before as it could possibly be.

Then he gently pushed her head down onto his shoulder.

"I was so wrong, my love — so wrong. When you came to me, when you held me as you did, you seemed to break down all the misery of years. You've killed all that fear I had, you've made me feel — I can't tell you, my love, I can't tell you. Holding you as I did then, touching you, it was as though — as though we were one person. Not two people battening on each other — one person. You and me, together. We — belonged," and then he threw his head back and laughed with pure joy. "It's all right, Harriet darling, it's *all right*! Can you understand? You've made it all right —"

And she breathed deeply, filling her body with the peace she had always looked for with him, feeling the same sense of being one person he had felt, for the first time in her life knowing what love would be, what it could offer her.

They sat together in the darkness, watching the window as the faint light of the moon disappeared as it sank behind the trees, letting the peace and silence of the old house wash over them.

Then, gently, with infinite tenderness, he carried her across the silent hallway, back to her own bed, to lay her softly on the pillow, to kiss her eyes, her mouth, her cold cheeks, wrapping her in love and gentleness.

"Goodnight my darling," he murmured. "Goodnight. Soon we won't ever say goodnight again, my love — we'll never leave each other. Not yet, my love — not yet for either of us. We — aren't the sort of people to spoil things for each other, are we? Not now. But soon — we'll be married, Harriet darling — and then it will be all right —"

And Harriet smiled up at him in the darkness, and with a soft laugh in her throat murmured, "All come right — just like algebra —" and she fell asleep as suddenly as a baby.

ISIS publish a wide range of books in large print, from fiction to biography. A full list of titles is available free of charge from the address below. Alternatively, contact your local library for details of their collection of ISIS large print books.

Details of ISIS complete and unabridged audio books are also available.

Any suggestions for books you would like to see in large print or audio are always welcome.

ISIS

7 Centremead
Osney Mead
Oxford OX2 0ES
(01865) 250333